T0071909

LOVE AT FIRST STING

Also by Alison Tyler

Best Bondage Erotica
Best Bondage Erotica 2
Exposed
Got a Minute?
The Happy Birthday Book of Erotica
Heat Wave: Sizzling Sex Stories
Luscious: Stories of Anal Eroticism
The Merry XXXmas Book of Erotica
Red Hot Erotica
Slave to Love
Three-Way
Caught Looking (with Rachel Kramer Bussel)
A Is for Amour
B Is for Bondage
C Is for Coeds
D Is for Dress-Up

LOVE AT FIRST STING

SEXY TALES OF EROTIC RESTRAINT

EDITED BY
ALISON TYLER

CLEIS
PRESS

Copyright © 2007 by Alison Tyler.

All rights reserved. Except for brief passages quoted in newspaper, magazine, radio, or television reviews, no part of this book may be reproduced in any form or by any means, electronic or mechanical, including photocopying or recording, or by information storage or retrieval system, without permission in writing from the publisher.

Published in the United States by Cleis Press Inc., P.O. Box 14697, San Francisco, California 94114.

Printed in the United States.
Cover design: Scott Ideleman
Cover photograph: Roman Kasperski
Text design: Frank Wiedemann
Cleis Press logo art: Juana Alicia
First Edition.
10 9 8 7 6 5 4 3 2 1

ACKNOWLEDGMENTS

The most important bindings, I've learned over the years, are the ties of friendship. Thanks go to Felice Newman and Frédérique Delacoste; Violet Blue and Thomas S. Roche; Barbara Pizio and Adam Nevill; and SAM.

The great art of life is sensation,
to feel that we exist, even in pain.

—Lord Byron

Contents

INTRODUCTION: CAGED LUST

Love is a dangerous game.

No doubt about it.

From the moment your eyes meet, until that first touch, first kiss, first tryst on the living room floor, your emotions run ragged. Your heart races. Every look burns with intensity. Every statement is loaded, filled with double meanings. You hear things differently. You speak in a brand-new language.

But love in a pain-pleasure relationship—well, that just ratchets things up another notch. His hand on the back of your neck is no longer the prelude to a sweet caress. It's the move before he puts you in your place, drops you to your knees, shows you who's in charge. Her fingernails, spade shaped, painted strawberry-red, are lovely to look at, especially when they dig their way down your naked skin, leaving marks you'll admire for days to come. Echoes, reminders of your night together.

Even the most mundane items in your household become possible sex toys—a wood-backed hairbrush can whip a naughty ass as easily as taming a stubborn hairdo. A handkerchief becomes a blindfold, a gag, a symbol to let others know exactly what you crave.

And what *do* you crave?

That Ping-Pong paddle, carelessly tossed on the bedside table.

The steel handcuffs, waiting for use in the bottom of your purse.

The leather belt that he's casually, oh so casually, draped over the chair, where you'll look at it all day long, and worry, and wonder, and plan, and hope. You'll walk past the chair, trying not to gaze at the leather hanging there. But you'll fail. You'll stroke the cold metal buckle, you might even double up the belt and let a blow hit your thigh. Gently at first, then a bit harder. And harder. So you'll know what it's going to feel like later. You'll be ready.

Ready for your fantasies to come true.

Because that's what the stories in this collection are all about: truth. The true pleasure of getting what you want. What you need. The true undeniable relief of being able to bare your soul—as well as your skin—to the hands of another. Or to be the one in charge. To be responsible for grabbing that belt. For reaching back. For making the first strike.

So lick your finger and get ready to turn the page, to enter the dark secret love of those who dabble in lust in cages and pain-tinged pleasure.

Alison Tyler
May 2007

INTO THE WOODS

Shanna Germain

Rebecca had dozed almost the whole way, just the way she liked. Bare feet up on the dashboard, sun slanting in the side window to warm her shoulder and her thigh. Her body dreaming to the rattle and hum of the truck.

When the rattle and hum changed to clunks, Rebecca woke but didn't open her eyes. This was her favorite moment: right before she knew where they were. Gerald took her somewhere new once a month, but it was always a surprise. She liked surprises, liked the way the trips kept their relationship new.

The trips weren't the only thing that kept their relationship new. The sex too…she smiled at the memory of the last trip they'd taken together. The hotel room was so fancy, the sheets so soft, she'd asked Gerald to bind her in them, as much of her as he could, before he fucked her.

She felt Gerald's hand on her thigh. Her smile had given her away. "Morning, sleepyhead," he said.

"Morning," she said. She kept her eyes closed a moment

longer, taking in the sounds and smells. The sun was gone off her shoulder now. Bumpy road beneath her, no other sounds of traffic or people. The air coming through the half-open window smelled green and fresh. Somewhere away from the city, but that's as much as she could tell. She should have known when Gerald had driven up the driveway in Aaron's truck.

Aaron was Gerald's best friend, and as far as Rebecca knew, they'd been friends since they were little kids. They'd even roomed together in college, which must be where they'd picked up their habit of sharing things. They were always borrowing each other's tools and vehicles. For this little trip, Gerald had traded their city-bred Honda for Aaron's big Ford.

Rebecca had liked Aaron the first time she met him, with his white-blond surfer's hair and his quick laugh. It was a good thing, she often teased Gerald. She'd never date a guy whose friends she didn't like. He was cute too. She'd been on the lookout for a girl-friend for him forever, but so far, he hadn't shown much interest.

Gerald gave her thigh another squeeze and Rebecca opened her eyes. Trees lined both sides of the road, so tall that she couldn't see the sky.

"Wow," she said. "Where are we?"

Gerald's big laugh filled the truck.

"I was hoping you'd ask," he said. "Umpqua National Forest. You like?"

She moved closer to him. His skin always smelled like cedar shavings and wood glue from the furniture shop where he worked. "I like," she said.

"Just wait," he said. His voice held that hint of mischief that she knew meant sex. Sex and something new. She shifted on the seat, aware of how quickly her body responded. Sometimes all she had to do was think about fucking him, or remember fucking him, and she'd be wet.

The trees came in closer, hemming them into the road. Rebecca watched them in silence. She knew better than to ask what the plan was. Gerald liked to surprise her almost as much as she liked to be surprised.

When he took a left onto a bumpy dirt road, Rebecca had to raise her eyebrow and look over at him. Gerald took his hand off her thigh to maneuver the truck around the big holes in the dirt. She still didn't ask, but they sure were in the middle of nowhere. And it was chillier than she was dressed for, in the white miniskirt and blue tank that Gerald had laid out for her that morning. She wrapped her arms around her shoulders and shivered a little.

The truck started climbing, almost nose in the air. Rebecca swallowed, trying to ease the pressure in her ears. Soon, the truck leveled out and they were beyond or above the trees—she couldn't tell which. Everything opened up around them, into rolling meadows of wildflower. The air grew warmer. White-capped mountains rose in the distance on all sides. She hadn't slept that long, but it was like she was in another country. She couldn't believe this was a place you could drive to from their house.

"Jesus, Gerald, it's beautiful. How did you find it?"

"That's my little secret," he said, which is what he always said when she asked how or why or where. And it also let her know something else: that he was feeling mischievous. No wonder he'd had her put on her heeled summer sandals and a pair of cherry-printed panties that didn't even begin to cover the curves of her ass.

She wiggled in the seat, still trying to ease the pressure she was already feeling between her legs. Gerald didn't say anything, but he must have noticed, because he grinned out the front window like he had a secret.

Gerald took another turn, driving along a path so faint that

Rebecca wondered if they were supposed to be there. When he stopped, she saw a picnic table and a ring of campfire stones. Camping then. She'd never been.

When they'd both gotten out and stretched, she came around and hugged him. "I didn't know you knew how to camp," she said to his shoulder.

"Oh, I don't," Gerald teased. "I thought you did."

"Very funny," she said.

Gerald held her at arm's length, like he was seeing her for the first time. She liked the way that he often studied her. Sometimes, when he tied her up, he'd just stand and watch her forever before he touched her.

But now he shook her. Hard. She gasped, and then felt a hot flare of anger in her chest.

"What was that—"

"This is what you wear for camping?" he asked. "Don't you know there are ticks? Snakes? It's dangerous out here."

She wrapped her arms around her shoulders and shivered. Gerald was dressed in jeans and hiking boots, a long-sleeved shirt.

"But you told me—" she started, and then she saw that dark thing in Gerald's hazel eyes. And she realized he'd set her up for this, that he'd planned this whole thing. He was going to fuck her here, in the middle of nowhere. He was going to punish her for a choice that she didn't even make. And she was going to let him.

The pressure between her thighs increased. Her panties were suddenly too tight, digging into her tender insides. She put her head down, looked at her pearly-painted toes, shiny against the meadow grass. "I'm sorry," she said.

Gerald tugged at her little skirt like he was trying to make it cover her thighs. His voice was softer. "This isn't going to work," he said. "It's too dangerous. You'll have to change into something else."

She scuffed the ground with her sandal, unsure. "But...I didn't bring anything else," she said.

Gerald raised her chin, made her look at him. "Then you'll have to borrow something of mine," he said. "Okay?"

He was asking about more than the clothes. He was asking her permission to move forward with this scene, this scene that he'd been planning for who knew how long. She was nervous, all this space around her. There wasn't anyone else here, but they were in the wide-open. It wasn't anything like the hotel room, or the other places Gerald had taken her.

But her body knew, and she didn't hesitate. "Okay, Gerald."

"Okay, *Sir*," he said.

Sir? She wasn't sure about that one. Rebecca swallowed. His eyes were still his eyes, the smart, sexy eyes she'd fallen in love with. He didn't blink, and she remembered how those lashes would sweep her belly with butterfly kisses in the mornings.

She wanted to tuck her hands between her thighs, both for comfort and to ease the ache she was feeling.

"Okay, Sir," she said.

He nodded, then walked around to the back of the pickup and opened the cap.

"Skirt off first," he said, not looking at her.

"What? Here?" She said it before she thought.

Gerald stood up straighter, taller. Before he spoke, his mouth was a straight line. "There's nobody here Bec, just you and me." The words sounded reassuring, but Rebecca knew that they weren't meant to be. Gerald was just laying down the rules.

Her safeword was on the tip of her tongue. All she had to do was say it. She'd said it once before, when Gerald had wanted to fuck her bent over the car on a busy street. She'd chickened out at the thought of being so exposed. She'd said the word. Gerald had squeezed her thigh and told her it was okay. But she'd always regretted it, not taking the chance. Maybe Gerald knew that, maybe he was offering her another go.

She looked around at the meadow. A few butterflies flitted from flower to flower, but Gerald was right. There wasn't anyone else here. She put her fingers against the side of her skirt. For a moment, her fingers felt too cold to undo the zipper. But Gerald's eyes warmed her, and she slid the zipper down. She carefully stepped out of her skirt, grateful he'd had her wear panties. At least they covered a bit of her ass.

When Gerald held out his hand, she folded her skirt and put it on his palm.

"Panties too," he said.

She should have known he wouldn't let her off that easy. She slid her panties down. The air against her skin was cool, but not cold. Still, she shivered. She knew Gerald was watching her while she bent. She stepped out of her panties and folded them before handing them over.

Gerald took her clothes and then rummaged in the back of the truck. While she waited for Gerald to hand her a new outfit—whatever it was that he'd picked out for her, she was sure it was some skimpy thing—she tried to cover her naked ass with her hands.

He saw her and laughed. Then he gave the bottom of one cheek a squeeze, letting her know just how much of it was visible, even through her spread fingers.

"First of all, you've got too nice of an ass to cover it up," he said.

Instead of clothes, he held out a canvas bag.

"And second of all, I don't actually have anything for you to wear," he said. "At least not yet. But if you get this tent set up before Aaron gets here, I might be able to find you something."

"Before..." She had trouble getting the words out.

Gerald looked at her as though he'd said something perfectly normal.

"Aaron's coming to spend the night," he said. That grin again. It made her insides feel soft and whooshy. "That was his trade for loaning me the truck."

Rebecca pinched her legs together and tried to think. Gerald had never introduced someone else to their weekends. She didn't know how that made her feel. Nervous as all hell, yes, but also aroused. Her pulse beat hard between her thighs.

Without waiting for her response, Gerald held out the canvas bag. "The tent," he said. And his voice held nothing but command.

Rebecca had never even slept in a tent before, much less put one together. She didn't know how long she had, and she didn't want to ask. Just as she reached for the canvas bag, Gerald let it slide from his fingers.

"Pick it up," he said.

Gerald leaned against the truck, watching. She bent, keeping her knees almost straight, the way he liked. She tried to forget that she was mooning the whole Umpqua forest in the process. Still, his quiet groan of appreciation made it easier and when Rebecca came back up, she wiggled her ass just a little.

"Over there," Gerald said. His voice was already slightly hoarse. "Where it's flat."

Rebecca grinned, but kept her face turned away. She didn't want Gerald to see how much she loved the effect she had on him, how easy she could create changes in his body. When they'd first started dating, and she asked for him to tie her, he'd obliged. And for a long time, she'd thought he was just doing it for her. But now she knew him well enough to know that he loved it as much as she did, loved seeing her vulnerable and begging for it.

At the flat spot, she pulled the tent out of the canvas bag. It was a mess of fiberglass poles and colored bungees and material. No directions. Oh Jesus, Rebecca thought, she was fucked here. There was no way she was going to get this thing together.

She tried to take the hollow poles apart, but they were hooked together with rubber bands or something inside, and they snapped back in place, getting even more tangled. Gerald was watching her. She couldn't see him, but her mind told her all she needed to know: he was still leaning back against the truck, his arms folded, just watching. Watching and waiting.

Fumbling with the poles while worrying about her bare ass was no easy task. One of the poles fell to the ground, hitting a rock with a loud ping.

Even without turning around, she knew Gerald was coming. She bent down fast to retrieve the fallen pole. But Gerald was faster, on her before she could stand back up. His zipper pressed into her ass. He bent over with her, so that she was beneath him and he was the one who came up with the pole in his hand.

His lips were against her ear. "I'm sure I don't need to tell you that this equipment is expensive," he said. "And here you are, throwing it on the ground."

"Gerald, I—"

He brought the tent pole against her throat, just hard enough to stop the rest of her sentence.

Rebecca swallowed. They'd played a lot of games, but this was the first time he'd used his strength on her like this. It scared her a little. But it also made her insides so soft. The world outside went away and it was just Gerald and her, just her pulse beating hard against the pole.

Gerald moved the pole down her neck, toward her chest. "Was there something you wanted to say?"

It wasn't a question, but Rebecca shook her head. The press of his zipper grew harder, until she could feel the outline of his cock against her ass. She tried not to squirm against it, even though she wanted to.

Gerald slid the pole down and ran the cold material over her breasts. Rebecca shivered, loving the feel of the hard pole against her nipples. Gerald must have seen her reaction because he increased the pressure, moved the pole up and down until her nipples were dark pink. They burned from the motion. Her breath stuttered out.

Gerald dropped the pole away from her body and reached around with his empty hand. He dipped one finger inside her. She was surprised how easy he went in, up to the first knuckle.

"Wet already, I see," he said into her ear.

Her cheeks flared crimson despite the cool air as a second finger slid inside her, and wiggled with the first. She couldn't help it; she let her head fall back with a sigh against Gerald's shoulder.

Gerald started speaking, moving his fingers inside her in time to his words.

"You know, the purpose of the tent is to keep us from getting wet." He was toying with her. Holding her to his body by the movement of his fingers. "But now you're already wet, so we have a bit of a problem, don't we?"

She nodded, and realized too late it wasn't what he wanted. The tent pole caressed the inside of her leg, moved toward her center.

"Don't we?" he asked again.

"Yes, Sir," she said, her voice vibrating in time to his fingers moving inside her. He raked his thumb over her clit, hard enough to empty her lungs. She pressed against the calloused flesh, aching.

But Gerald gave his big laugh and pulled his fingers out of her, leaving her wet and hollow. He put his fingers to her lips and she sucked him in. Her own tangy and sweet taste flooded her tongue. He let her suckle him just long enough for her to wish it was his cock in her mouth, and then he pulled his fingers from her lips.

When he put his hand against the back of her neck, she knew he meant for her to touch the ground. And so she did, with her hands first, and then as he bent her even more, with the tips of her long hair.

She stayed that way, looking at her pale fingers spread out on the ground. Her dark hair rustled over the yellow grasses.

"Hands to your ankles," he said. "And open your legs." Gerald tapped the inside of her thighs with the pole as he spoke. It didn't hurt, but she saw it had potential. She quickly spread her legs and then wrapped her hands tight to her bare ankles.

The bungee cords made loops, binding her wrists to her ankles. And then, as if Gerald was afraid she was going to run away like that, he wrapped a bungee loosely from ankle to ankle, shackling her. The stretchy material gave her the impression that she could break free, but when she tried to wiggle in the bonds, she knew she had underestimated it.

"Okay?" Gerald asked. It was his real voice. It let her know that he was outside of his comfort zone too, something that rarely happened. The thought gave her strength. It also made the buzz between her legs louder.

Instead of answering, she wiggled her ass at him. It was a bold move, and she knew it, but she couldn't help herself.

Gerald's voice was more growl than anything. And then there was the heat, thin and hot against the back of her thigh. The long sear of the pole nearly set her off balance. She gripped her ankles tighter trying to stay upright.

Gerald was using the tent pole. She realized it as soon as the second strike hit, right on the outside of the curve of her ass. At home, Gerald favored his hand or a paddle. This pain was different. Not a flat slap of pain, but a thin laser that seared into her flesh.

He brought the pole against the other side of her ass. Another strip of laser. Rebecca took a deep inhale, trying to right herself against the throbbing. Her ass, between her legs—her whole lower half felt like it was on fire.

Knowing Gerald, her ass was now perfectly matched, with a long, pink welt on each side. When he started like this, it meant he was going to work his way down from the top of her ass to the bottom, flipping from one cheek to the other until her ass was striped like a zebra. It meant that before he was finished, he was going to use that tent pole on her clit.

She shuddered, even before Gerald brought the pole down on her skin again. He must have seen her movement, because he put his force behind the next swing. The pole gave a short tight whistle and then landed.

Again and again, the strokes came down, getting closer to her clit until every inch of her ass felt scalded. The pain was there, but she could barely feel it over the throbbing of her clit. She didn't think she could stand it another minute if he didn't touch her.

Seeming to sense this, Gerald put the pole between her legs and brought it up against her clit. She gritted her teeth and tried not to cry out. She knew that any sounds would increase her punishment. But on the second hit, she squealed just a little. Her clit was so raw and ripe that every movement brought her closer to the edge. She couldn't ever remember wanting to come so badly.

"Please, Gerald, please..." As soon as she said it, she knew.

He stopped. Oh god, the empty ache was worse than the pain. She knew what she needed to say, but she couldn't bring herself to say it.

"Please, what?" he asked. He still didn't touch her. Her clit boomed against the cool air until she thought she couldn't bear it.

When she finally said it, it was so quiet that she was afraid he hadn't heard. She was afraid her words got lost in her hair and the position.

But Gerald must have heard at least the "Sir" part, because he pressed the pole against her. The material, which she knew was warm from striking her skin, rolled back and forth over her clit. She gasped at this new sensation, the solid pressure and roll of it.

Gerald kept rubbing the pole back and forth over her clit in the same motion she would have used with her fingers, if her fingers were free. He was bringing her so close, so close.

"You're not going to come, are you?" he said.

She wasn't sure, but she shook her head anyway. The only sound was her own hitched breath and the tips of her hair brushing the grass.

Gerald pressed his blue-jeaned cock against her ass and kept going like he didn't notice her response. "Because if you come, I'll have to leave you like this until Aaron gets here," he said. "I can just imagine him driving up, expecting a few birds and bees and finding…"

When Gerald said *Aaron*, she had an instant picture of him in her head. She couldn't help it, she imagined him touching her, bending his blond head to lick her nipples while Gerald rubbed the tent pole against her clit.

She had to shake the image out of her head, so she wouldn't come. But her body kept moving of its own accord, pressing and rubbing against the pole that Gerald was holding.

Gerald didn't take the pole away. He just kept sliding it back and forth over her clit while he talked. "...Finding you here, dripping. All wrapped up in pieces of his tent. Naughty little girl."

At that, she couldn't stop it anymore. She couldn't even pretend to be in control as her pussy clenched at the sides of the pole, looking for something to draw in. Gerald was nearly fucking her, even though he was still dressed, his zippered cock rubbing back and forth across her already sensitive skin. She loved coming like this, the way the world slid away and she was just the burn of her ass and her clit, an exhale of "oh, oh..."

And then it was over, and her legs shook so hard she wasn't sure she could stay upright, but Gerald held her up with the pole and his hands until she stopped trembling.

As soon as she stopped, Gerald stepped away, leaving her wet and bent, wrung like a rag. It wasn't just her ass that was exposed; she felt like her desires were out there in the open now too.

She stayed that way, looking at her pale fingers spread out on the ground. At dark hair touching the yellow grasses. She couldn't see Gerald. Couldn't feel him either. Her mouth wanted to cry out to him, to hear him answer, no matter what her punishment would be. But she refused to break that easy.

She inhaled, trying to tell herself she could be doing yoga. Trying to tell herself to forget that she was half-naked, her entire lower body open to the world. For a moment, she was content to bend there, in the silence. Knowing that she and Gerald were alone in all this bigness, that he was watching her from somewhere. That he'd be back any second to take care of her.

And then she heard the sound of their Honda, coming slowly up the dirt road behind her.

TORN

Vida Bailey

Jen had been tutoring Marcus for about a year. He was just twenty. She was nearing the end of that decade and lonely. The lessons were no hardship for Jen. In the absence of a boyfriend, she had grown to look forward to their weekly hour together as she would a date. Her initial observation that he was extremely attractive had grown into something more urgent. She found subtle excuses to touch him.

As the hour of his arrival approached, Jen would pass the hall window, hoping to catch an extra glance at him as he walked up her drive. She took pleasure in opening the door of her house to him, and welcoming him in.

Just before his exams they'd had an encounter. It was a quick Shake 'n' Bake of a tryst, a spank and wank, if you will. On his way into the study he had bent to talk to her terrier.

"Hey, Rags, hey little dude. How are ya?" His combats rode down to reveal the band of his tighty whities and a tattoo above that, an intricate pattern spreading out from the base of his spine. Jen had to clutch the door frame, weak-kneed. But his homework was less impressive.

"So did you get to do the essay plan we discussed?"

His usual excuses surfaced again. "I just didn't get time, I'll have it next week, I will."

Frustration replaced the wave of desire. "Do you want to get into University, Marcus?"

A shrug. "I can't really deal with the thought of another four years of school." Yet here he was. Trying to do the right thing, but scared to try in case he failed.

"It looks like we're wasting each other's time, then. And you're wasting your mother's money."

"I hear enough of that from her." His light voice grew testy. She tried a different tack. Hand on hip, she risked a joke.

"Get it together, Marcus. I'm not your mother. Don't talk to me like that. I'd swear you were looking for a spanking."

To her astonishment, he had turned to her, eyes bright, and his tongue darted out to moisten his lips. "If you think it will help." He arched an eyebrow.

Jen's armpits prickled and she felt her pulse begin to drum. Where was self-preservation when she needed it? The little demon on her shoulder pushed her better judgment firmly out of the way. Her internal struggle ended when she ordered him to bend over the desk.

"Trousers down, Marcus, we may as well do this properly."

He'd obeyed quickly enough, eager fingers unbuckling his belt. He shivered when she rested her hand lightly on his ass, giving him time to back out, to laugh it off. When he turned and locked eyes with her, she read only excitement there.

"I *do* need a spanking, Jen."

So she had obliged, landing smack after firm smack on his buttocks as he braced himself against the desk. She'd finished the spanking by grabbing a light wooden ruler and rubbing it against his hot cheeks.

"Have you learned your lesson?"

"I...yes, I..." She could see he wasn't sure how to answer; the ruler sliding to and fro on the cotton of his pants was distracting him, as was his erection, straining his waistband. He rubbed himself on the edge of the desk and closed his eyes. She marveled that he was so into this. She brought the ruler down on his ass, snapping it in a fast series of little slaps that she knew would sting his tenderized skin. When she stopped, he straightened and reached back to rub his rear. It was her turn to raise her eyebrows.

"Well?"

"I'm sorry I snapped. And I'm sorry about this." He grinned and gestured to his cock. "I can't go home like this."

He was right. He couldn't. She'd crossed the line when she made him undress. But she tried, she paid lip service to common sense. "You know I can't. This isn't—it's too much to ask of you. If I were in your place, I wouldn't be able to stop myself telling my friend I just got it on with a teacher. And then he'd tell his mother, and she'd tell your mother. And I'd be in the papers."

But it was too late. It was like putting the ice cream back in the freezer when she knew she was going to eat it all in half an hour.

"I know, Jen, Jesus, I won't. I wouldn't tell." Ignoring her inner warning voice, her hand reached into his briefs to encircle silky skin and it didn't take long to help him find his pleasure. She watched him come across the notes spread on the table, his eyes squeezed tightly shut. The image would continue to flare in her mind for days.

Before he left, his "Thanks, Jen" had been a little more

heartfelt than usual. She wasn't sure if he understood the import of his promises of silence. She prayed that he did.

She pictured his body bent over the table where they worked, her palm connecting with his tight white briefs, the slight tremble in his athlete's thighs. Closing her eyes, she could feel the rove and squeeze of her hand on his buttock, the smooth skin of his back. What got to her most were his arms, strong and lithe. She thought the T-shirt tan line made the flesh of his bicep seem more vulnerable, smooth as it was. His bitten nails matched her own and reminded her that there was insecurity buried beneath his cocky demeanor.

What she wanted most was to be enfolded in the protective circle of those arms, to feel his heartbeat against her cheek through his chest. To cheer at the side of the pitch as he competed, or watch him laze on the grass, one knee cocked, in the sunshine, smiling a smile that was just for her. In truth, she wanted to be young again, just out of school and cherished. She slapped the nostalgic fantasy away. She was something else entirely, a teacher, an older woman, a disciplinarian. She was grateful to have this boy in her life at all.

She wondered if he would come back again the next week and was almost surprised when he appeared, loping up the drive with his shoulders tensed, the way he always did. He was sulky and sullen. He wouldn't concentrate.

"Did you have a good week, then?"

"Yeah."

"So what are we working on today?"

"Whatever."

Jen persevered. "Marcus, will you look at me? You need to back that point up with a solid quote if it's going to hold up."

"All right! I know! I'm doing it!" Amused, Jen had an insight into what it *would* feel like to be his mother: a mixture of

fierce pride and screaming frustration. Then she realized what
he was doing.

"Well, Marcus, we have two choices here. Either you can go
home and work on your own, or you can go upstairs to the bedroom, take off your shirt and put your hands on the wall above
your head and wait for me."

She stood, hand on hip. He didn't look at her as he left the
room, his books lying askew on the table.

She left him to wait a little. The idea of him standing, hands
planted on the wall in her room, was tantalizing. After gathering
a few things, she entered and drank in the sight of his slim torso,
naked to the waist. Each vertebra was visible on his smooth, pale
back. The tattoo stood out starkly against his skin. It was again
framed by the white of the underwear that peeked above the top
of his low-slung jeans. She traced his backbone with a finger,
from hairline to tat, and delighted in his shivered response.

"Move over, Marcus," she breathed, maneuvering him to
stand beneath a bracket fixed on the wall. Slowly she ran her
hand up his side, catching his wrist in a cuff that dangled from a
bracket on the wall. She did the same for the other arm, running
her fingers up his side, rib by rib, causing him to break out in
goose bumps. She stopped just above his armpit and floated his
other arm up to join the first.

Jen stepped in close and sucked a kiss onto Marcus's shoulder. She snaked one arm round his chest and pinched his nipple.
His skin was softer than she expected, and warm. One finger
followed the gentle fuzz of pubic hair down to the top button
of his jeans. She listened to his breathing deepen with each button, heard him catch his breath as she released the last one. His
jeans slid away without resistance and she paused to absorb the
glorious picture of him, stripped to his underwear and bound to
her wall.

She reached into the leg of his briefs, stroking the smooth skin and letting the elastic snap back into place. Sliding her fingers through the valley of his taut buttocks, she reached beneath him to cup his balls and rub. He braced himself and swallowed, his muscles tense. She could imagine his Adam's apple moving as his head dipped forward. A noise escaped his lips, half sigh, half groan. It sounded delightful, so light, heralding such desperate pleasure. Sweet boy.

"Spread, Marcus, nice and wide," she ordered, slapping his inner thigh. He obediently moved into position, his muscles standing out. Without any warning, she smacked his ass with the flat of her hand, moving from one side to the other on the fleshiest part of his buttocks, feeling the heat, the sting in her own palm. Caught off guard, he gasped and twisted, as if trying to avoid the blows without really moving. She stopped when a rose blush crept past the sides of his underwear, working its way to his upper thighs. She rubbed his ass, easing the sting, then pressed herself to him.

"Will this help you work harder, Marcus?" she whispered in his ear. The heat from his spanked buttocks seeped into her crotch. She pushed against him a little more firmly, reaching to twist his nipple sharply.

She could hear him fight to keep his voice low and steady.

"Yes! Yes."

She thought about the stubble on his jaw that shone golden in the light and wanted to turn him around, stroke it. Not yet.

Jen inched his briefs down over his ass, loving the contrast of the red flush against his milky skin. She could see him feel her gaze, the sweat breaking out under his arms, on his back. She licked at his shoulder, spreading lube on her fingers while his attention was on her tongue, her hot mouth kissing the sweat away. She pushed his legs apart again and rimmed his asshole with a light touch, waiting until he relaxed. Then she pulled away so his ass would have to follow. He begged for more with the press of his pelvis into her hand. Her finger slipped into his heat, and the thrill of possessing him and his gasp of "Oh god!" made her dizzy.

With a groan, he pumped his hips and his head fell back. She eased her finger out of him and cradled his balls again, her thumb against his hole.

"Jen..."

"What, Marcus?"

"Don't stop. Please..."

"Don't stop *what*, pretty boy?"

He took a breath.

"Your fingers, Jen, in me. Don't stop."

She reached up and stroked his bobbing Adam's apple, then rasped her left thumb over his cheek. He sighed as she returned her finger to his loosened ass, and then added another, slowly. Marcus stayed quiet, but his breath grew ragged.

She stepped back and away, quickly squirting lube on the plug she had ready for him. It was cold. He stiffened and pulled away, scared. Jen tisked and picked up her wide black hairbrush.

"I thought you were asking for this, Marcus. You've let me tie you up, you're naked in my room. Are you just messing with me again, just wasting my time, again?" She touched his cock for the first time, gripping it, finding it hard despite his nerves. At the same time she slapped the brush down several times, right over his asshole. "This is all about you behaving, Marcus. Don't disappoint me further," she whispered in his ear. He shook his head, disoriented and overwhelmed.

"No, Jen. Sorry, I didn't mean to." His voice was rough, the pain showed in it. She might have been moved by it if it hadn't been for the insistent throbbing in her crotch.

"Do you trust me, Marcus?" He nodded. *Smack.* "Do you trust me?"

"I trust you."

"Right. No more nonsense then." She patted him, spread his cheeks again, shifted her left hand back to his balls and slowly pushed the plug up into him.

"Good boy. That's it." He breathed deeply, adjusting to the fullness, the pressure. She tapped the plug's base and spoke into his ear again.

"Now Marcus, I want to give you something to remember this lesson by. I want you to feel this sting as you sit and study, and let it remind you to focus, to do the work for me."

The chain clicked as she pulled the cuffs from the hook. He meekly followed her to the bed and knelt at her command. She relocked his wrists behind him. She stepped away from him and pulled the belt from his discarded jeans.

"On your face." Her voice was harsh. The chain left just enough slack for him to kneel with his face in the pillows. She doubled the strap and pushed his cheeks apart, slapping at the plug with gentle strokes, working up to harder swings on the cleft of his ass. She slapped stripes across his already crimson cheeks, the tops of his thighs. But she returned each time to the plug.

"Please, Jen..." She heard a soft plea, tears in his voice. But he hadn't moved, other than to writhe and thrust away from the slaps of the leather. Not stopping the strokes, she reached under him to rub the head of his cock between a light finger and thumb. She played the belt against the plug base, knowing how the smacks were vibrating through him. She felt his cock surge, saw his hips begin to pump and then, taking one last slap, he covered her hand in his come, his voice incoherent in release. She let him breathe a minute, then ordered him to the floor. He knelt, his wet eyes cast down. When she pressed her hand to his lips he licked it clean. She thumbed the tears from under his lashes, unable to resist kissing his mouth, pressing her lips to the salt of tears and come.

Jen stood in front of him as he knelt, his wrists bound behind him, pulling his shoulders back. The position revealed the interlocked curves inked onto the pale underside of his arm. Slowly, he let his head rest on her hip bone, exhausted and nuzzling. His forehead was warm against her, damp with sweat.

She had been going to send him home. She couldn't, not now. She stepped back, raised her skirt inch by inch and then reached for the back of his head. It made so much sense to guide his face to her cunt. She held him there while he kissed the cotton of her wet panties. Impatient, she pulled them off and pressed his mouth to her. She put one foot on the bed frame and he pushed his tongue into her, licking, eyes closed. His tongue felt muscular and agile as he pressed further in, his breath warm against her. She angled her pelvis down and he licked her clitoris in strong sweeps, no tickling teasing, just the forceful push of his tongue over and over.

"Marcus…" She was about to tell him to suck her but he needed no instruction. Fettered as he was, his lips closed over her clit and pulled fiercely, drinking her. She felt the scrape of his perfect white teeth grazing her clit, his hungry mouth raising the burn and slam of a searing orgasm. He didn't stop until her cries had died away. She pulled him back by the hair, fist locked at the nape of his neck. The fingers of her other hand petted his face. She fell to her knees, thighs pressed together, and reached up to kiss him, his mouth slick with his come and her own taste.

His cock was coming up again. Jesus. That brought her back to her college boyfriends. She pushed the thought of really having him away. Marcus was never going to be hers, she didn't get to have him. She wanted him, so badly she could taste it—his arm thrown over her in sleep, her feet dipping into his bath, his cock stretching and driving her. No, Jen. What he had to give would not be enough. But tenderly she kissed him, leaning into him. Her lips and tongue-tip tested until her mouth locked over his, and her head swirled. In his aura, in the heat of him, she felt secure, right. She pulled back and reached behind him to release his arms. She stood abruptly, her skirt swishing back into place. She picked up his underwear, tucked it into the pocket of his jeans.

"You can go home without wearing these, and feel every thread of your jeans against those tender parts of yours. With every little chafe you'll remember your lesson."

She slapped his hands on the chest of drawers and pulled the plug from him, ignoring his sudden exhalation and the way his ass clenched on its emptiness. She walked out, leaving him to dress and return to his books.

Jen made it to the hall downstairs. She leaned against the wall and slid to the floor. She rested her chin on her knees and fiddled with her earring. She thought of her orgasm and a searing physical memory flashed through her. Shit. What was she going to do?

Marcus walked down the stairs. She watched his knees approaching, looked away as his crotch hove into view. He sat down beside her, gingerly, and leaned his head against hers for a second.

"Are you okay?" she asked, her voice dull. Fatigue robbed her of any interest in continuing the game.

He nodded. "My ass is killing me though."

She smiled. "Perhaps it will put the agony of studying into perspective."

"Yeah."

Her voice became brisk. "Right. How many weeks left? Two?

So will I see you next week?" He nodded. "Bring your books, and two essay plans. Time's running out, Exam Boy."

They stood, and moved to the door. She rested a light hand on his back as he walked out.

"And Marcus?"

"Yes?"

"If you don't have your work done next week"—he smirked suggestively but grew serious as she finished—"then there's nothing more I can do for you." He stared at her, then nodded. She hadn't been testing him, but his acceptance stung her none-theless. She wished he would argue, even just a little bit. But they both got it. There was no room for romance.

After he left she watched his back; his long legs walking down the lane, away. His stride was more careful than the one he had come with. He was tender. Tears rose in her eyes. If she could she would keep him tied, to her bed, to her body, to move within the circle of his warmth and have him smile a smile that was for her only, secret, teasing and possessive.

A tear traced its cold, saline path over her mouth and she pressed her hand to his kiss; felt it lingering, the scrape of his beard, the plush of his lips.

Torn, she was, and yearning.

WAGES OF PRIDE

Jen Cross

Denim and leather, tonight. Black boots leaving a heavy thud behind me as I walk. It's night in the Mission and all the lights are up, cutting cleanly through the fog and mist. Everything's awash in lust, including me. Tired of spending my nights alone at home, trying to forget how you tossed me aside, Daddy, I've come out on top of the night. I'm on the prowl.

There's a throng of baby girls hovering around the door of the bar, leaden with hope, boisterous talk and unfulfilled wishes. I suck on the tail end of my cigarette until I taste burned plastic on my tongue. Exhaling, I flick the butt into the street and make my way into the crowd of girls, glancing around to see if there's anyone interesting. One cute young butch has the attention of a high-femme drama queen who appears not to realize that the boy she's got her sights on is into other boys—I can tell by the way the butch draws her eyes across me. There's a punky femme dashed up against the brick wall, plastered and needing to be taken out of herself. Her eyes glaze me with her pain, and I look away. She looks too much like I feel and I can't pick up anyone else's pieces when I'm so shattered myself.

Sighing, I flick my ID at the bouncer and elbow my way into the packed room. No wonder everyone's outside—there're so many dykes in this tiny space that there's hardly any breathable air. I suck in my gut to avoid rubbing up against too many people, and manage, somehow, to work my way up to the bar. I find myself suddenly and sharply craving another cigarette, but I know that's just the fear under my libido, nudging me back out into the clouded night, toward my empty bed and hard heart. So I order a beer and lean up against the bar, scanning the crowd for any interesting faces. I get a couple raised eyebrows, but there's no one parading the bad intentions I'm looking for, the hot and hostile grimace that makes me curl my lip and squeeze my thighs together.

Three-quarters of an hour later, while nursing the beer and my disappointment, I'm jostled hard enough from behind that I spill what little is left in my bottle all over my pants. I turn sharply, ready to give a harsh reprimand to whoever's so drunk that they can't hold themselves steady, but napkins are already being thrust into my hands and the damp spot on my thigh mopped at before I can even make eye contact with the offender.

"Oh my gosh, I am so sorry," says the person attached to the bejeweled hand now resting firmly on my thigh. I look up, an irrepressible grin casting my face from admonishment to ac-quiescence and forgiveness. My interloper is a femme of the first order: tall and round, with bronze-charcoal skin and the kind of eyes that have historically driven butches to fisticuffs or drink, usually both. This is the closest I'm going to get to a hookup tonight, and this is precisely the sort of woman I'm *not* attracted to. At all. Damn it.

But at least it's something to do, better than staring at the heads and shoulders of denim-clad dykes surrounding me. And she's laughing so hard into her embarrassment that I can't help but laugh with her, assuring her that these jeans have seen a hell of a lot worse than a little beer. Her eyes flash for a second, but whatever cocking was going on with her guns disappears as soon as I take notice. She orders another round for herself and for me, in spite of my protests.

"It was only a little spill—please don't worry about it."

"Oh, no, come on—you've gotta walk around in the wet spot all night now," the woman chuckles. "The least I can do is buy you another. I'm Shirleen, by the way. What's your name?" she asks as she's settling up with the harried bartender, the cute butch I usually flirt with when things aren't so busy. Shirleen pours such a focused attention in my direction that before I realize it, I'm deep into my sob story—how my Daddy's left me because there was something I just wouldn't do. Sounds like some kind of twisted country love song.

Maybe it's the beer that has so blinded me to what's going on—or lust, 'cause I haven't really had that much to drink. I don't even see it coming when she says, piercing me with the sharpness of her gaze, "And what did Daddy want you to do, Jay?"

I freeze, caught like a goddamn deer in the headlights—or in someone's sights. "Oh shit," I mumble, trying to get out of this. I don't even have to look around—I know Daddy's here, lost in the thickness of the crowd. My cunt floods and my head starts to ache.

"You got me talking your ear off, Shirleen—uh, what brings you to this crazy place tonight?" I do my best to turn on my interested eyes, wondering if they come through the drunken haze of desire. But it doesn't work. She's locked and loaded. Her hand, which had been tickling sympathetic, sharp-tipped fingers up the back of my neck and along my shoulder blades, suddenly tightens in the thicket of my hair, bringing up a gasp that scalds my throat.

"Didn't I ask you a question, boy?"

Of course, I know my role. "Yes, Ma'am."

"And doesn't it constitute disobedience on your part to deliberately avoid answering me?"

Conversation quiets, as nearby patrons figure out what's going on and start paying attention. Shirleen's fingers manage to tighten in my short hair and she maneuvers my head to one side. My knees go weak.

"Yes, Ma'am."

"And what happens to disobedient little boys?" She's grinning slyly, holding my eyes with hers as she wraps her painted lips around her straw for a sip of her drink.

"They get a spanking?" announces some obnoxiously unhelpful bystander. I'd glare at them, if I could, but I'm already too far gone.

Shirleen glances at the folks to her right, indicating without a word that people should move away from the pool table. A space appears into which I am not so much flung as presented. She's taller than I am, especially in those platforms. Unsteady with nerves and need, I pull my own hair as she keeps steady, waiting for me to come to a standstill.

"Drop your pants, Jay," she says, her eyes glistening in the dark light of the bar and her lips twisted up at the edges with enjoyment.

"Oh, hell no." I am immediately appalled to realize that these words have escaped from my lips. The crowd around us lets out various exclamations of surprise and alarm. I find myself steeling into her. If she's come this far, Daddy surely has told her my safe word. Crap. After a moment or two of us staring at each other—facing off—Shirleen raises her eyes up, looking over my head.

"You. Get up on this table and hold her hands." Were it not for the boards over the pool table's flannel, that green fabric would've been shredded years ago after stunts like this. My arms are raised up over my head and held there by someone with more leverage and strength than I have at this moment.

"You were gonna get the benefit of your drawers, boy—but now I think you'll get it bare-assed." Shirleen meets the eyes of another femme, who seems all too glad to be involved in my public humiliation. This girl, a round-eyed redhead with a thin face and her hair up in uneven pigtails, her pale skin ruddy with drink and the heat of her desire, folds herself into a squat while she unbuckles my belt and lets my jeans fall to the floor, leaving my boxers for the moment so that everyone can see the ridiculous smiley faces covering my ass, as well as the cock poking out against the fabric. She slides back up, dragging her soft, thick tits along my naked legs, then against my chest. When I don't respond, she performs for the crowd, turning around to rub her ass against my dick. She catches the attention of one of the barbacks, but before I can see where that's going to lead, I'm brought back to my own present.

Shirleen eases the girl into the crowd, using the back of her hand and almost no effort, then grabs hold of my cock. "Planning on getting lucky tonight, were you, Jay?" The bar erupts in laughter. "Well, you got lucky, didn't you? Just not like you were planning."

My cheeks flush and I shudder in the wake of the adrenaline that washes through me. I continue pulling against the hands binding my wrists, and the girl holding my head—surely I'm butch enough to get away from a couple of femmes. I twist and turn, start getting pretty fucking obnoxious. I'm considering where a kick might be most effectively placed, when Shirleen leans in and whispers in her deep voice, "Keep it up, and I'll let them fuck you right here. With your very own cock that you've so thoughtfully provided. You want 'em all to know how wet this whole thing's got you, baby boy?"

I don't quite freeze, but I must register some sort of acquiescence on my face—a couple butches nearby chuckle in recognition.

"Turn around," Shirleen orders for everyone to hear, backing away from me. I do, so that I am facing the knees and thighs of the girl holding my hands.

"Look at her." And so I raise my eyes, meeting the strong-featured face of Carly, a femme top I'd snubbed at a party a few weeks ago, when this whole thing started.

Carly had wanted to have her bottom spank me in front of her. The bottom was a snotty bio-fag who'd been catty toward me all night, and had my hackles up. I tried to get Daddy not to make me do it, but she wasn't having any of my shit (she said). I knew how to get out of it, but instead of safewording, I told Carly she could spank me when hell froze over, and that went for any of her proxies as well. Livid, Daddy had handed me the end of the leash she'd had me on that night, a ten-dollar bill for a cab, and told me to go home. I was not to call or attempt to have any sort of contact; Daddy would get in touch with me if and when she was ready.

Oh.

There, towering above me, Carly smiles broadly. "Hey, Jay," she drawls, her straight black hair casting about those high cheekbones like bits of broken spiderweb. Carly's a bodybuilder when she's not busy annihilating butch egos. "Kinda chilly in here, isn't it?"

Shirleen releases my hair, and my scalp throbs into the emptiness. "This sure is fun, isn't it?" Carly giggles. It's that stupid lilting giggle that brought a wrinkle of disgust to my nose at that party, followed swiftly by the back of Daddy's hand to my cheek. I hold my face steady, carefully considering my answer, when I feel the elastic of my boxers dragging down over my ass and thighs. The cock snaps out from under the elastic front and hits the edge of the pool table with a *thwak*.

The crowd's agitated, needing to see something, and my ass was *something*, anyway. There are scattered cheers and impatient shouts of encouragement to "get the fuck on with it."

"You keep your eyes on her face while I do this, Jay—after all, it's her punishment, isn't it?"

I hold Carly's purple-tinted eyes as I choke out, "Yes, Ma'am."

"Carly?"

"Why, yes, Shirleen?" Carly answers with a big grin just for me.

"How many's she get?" Shirleen rubs her hot hands over my ass, calling my nerves to awareness. While this conversation goes on over my head, I wonder where Shirleen came from, and why I've never seen her around. Surely I'd remember a sweetly hostile, fiercely gorgeous black femme top at events.

"Let's say ten?" There are cheers and shouts of "More, more!" "Fifteen?" Same reaction. I half close my eyes, which, of course, she notices. "No—twenty-six," she says with finality, looking directly at me and then at Shirleen. "Thirteen's your lucky number, isn't it? Thirteen, then a break, then thirteen more, Shirleen."

"Somebody better help me keep count."

I think for a moment I'll be shrouded by the crowd's riotous counting, but no. The same helpful asshole who spoke up before says, "But isn't that her job?"

Carly's eyes narrow against the *Fuck you!* that creeps into mine, and she says, "Well, it sure is. Keep count, boy."

I take a deep breath and am just exhaling when Shirleen's hand lands hard and full on my left asscheek. "One," I announce into the silence, gritting my teeth. There's a pause as I brace for two.

"Really?" Carly says for the benefit of the bystanders, chewing on her bottom lip. "That's not really enough, is it? How 'bout, after the count, you thank your mommy?"

"And doesn't she have to ask for another?" offers Ms. Unhelpful. Carly's annoyed by this last interruption, though, and retorts, "Honey, I think you're getting too far into your own fantasy now, huh?" From the satisfied smirk that splashes across her face, I can see she received the embarrassed response she'd hoped for.

"Try again, baby boy. Start over."

Shirleen's hand lands with a sharp thud on my left cheek. "One. Thank you, Mommy," I say, watching Carly.

"Oh, louder, honey. They can't hear you in the back," says Shirleen from behind me. Another smack, landing precisely atop the first two.

"Two. Thank you, Mommy."

As Shirleen works into my punishment, no one laughs as I'd expected them to. Any chuckles I hear as my ass begins to burn, then sting, then just fucking hurt, come purely out of somebody's lust. Shirleen gives me no leeway, nailing each solid blow right on top of the same tenderized skin. By the count of thirteen, my left asscheek is swollen and raw. I grit my teeth and breathe deeply, figuring she'll move to the right side with her next stroke. But no.

"Thirteen," I gasp almost triumphantly. "Thank you, Mommy."

"You wanna take a minute and shake out your hand, Shirleen?" Carly asks, not really expecting a response. She squats down on her heels to lower her face to mine.

"You see, Jay, you coulda done this in private—but you're just a whore for an audience, aren't you?"

"Yes, Ma'am." I've got no idea if I'm agreeing with her because it's really true, or just to keep things moving. I wonder if my thighs are really as slick as it feels like they are. I'm about to find out, 'cause someone's got her hands between my legs.

"Oh, Carly," I hear. "We might have to get this baby a diaper." I lose awareness of the crowd's laughter as Shirleen's long, square-tipped nails push through the hot flesh of my labia and scrape gently across my clit. I catch my breath, ready to push back at her, so badly do I need to get fucked. But then she flattens the palm of her hand against my pussy, getting it soaked with my juice, which she then wipes off on my reddened ass. I can just make out my own scent through the dyke bar smells of beer, cigarette breath, and cologne. With my ass wet, it is suddenly cold, and a chill shudders through me.

Carly watches this halftime show, allowing her eyes to fall now and then to my lips, languidly raising those thickly lashed hazy orbs back to meet mine. "You ready to get this over with?"

A trick question. "I'm ready for whatever you have to give me, Ma'am."

She laughs sharply. "Isn't that what you told your Daddy?" She catches just the initial flash of my enraged embarrassment before she kisses me, pressing narrow lips and sharp tongue up against my waiting and swollen mouth. And just as I begin to feel the spasms of need infiltrate my thighs, Carly breaks the kiss abruptly, chuckling along with several bystanders as I fall forward when she stands up again, my desire pathetically apparent.

"Go on, Shirleen."

Another strike, on the still slightly wet skin of my oversensitive left cheek. My eyes go wide with pleading, but I say nothing except, "Fourteen—thank you, Mommy," in a voice that's high and tight.

Shirleen has strong hands. By the end I can feel nothing but the heavy burning of my ass. I feel as though one side of me is misshapen, the other side plain and ashen. Tears are hot in my eyes and I am wailing out the count, and my thanks. "Twenty-six," I groan, panting. "Th-thank you, Mommy." I pull at my arms, expecting to be released. But Carly does not let go.

"Oh, let's have one more," she says with a smooth smile. She could do this all night. I hold her gaze, resolutely defiant despite reddened cheeks and an ass that feels ready to split open with one more strike. I grunt and bite my lips when Shirleen hits me.

"Twenty-seven," I announce through clenched teeth. "Um, thank you, Mommy." It takes until thirty for them to break through to my tears and squeals.

Then the energy behind me shifts. I watch Carly's face for some hint of what's going on. But it isn't until I feel Daddy's hand at the small of my back and five more rapid-fire blows, bringing tears to flow down my face, that I am released of my anxiety and finally feel free.

Then, quiet in my ear: "Say 'thank you.' "

"Thank you, Daddy."

Pain where my earlobe is yanked closer to Daddy's hot mouth. "No."

"Thank you, Carly," I yelp as Daddy takes a handful of my tortured ass.

Carly winks at me, dropping my arm—now useless, of course. While I shake my limp limbs, wincing as the blood starts to move back through them, Daddy scrapes rough hands over my inflamed ass as she yanks up my jeans. I have to force myself not to twist away from her grasp.

"Go get my beer," Daddy whispers into my ear, her hand

firm on my neck. I have no idea where she might have left her beer, so I grab for the one Shirleen had ordered for me and hope for the best. Daddy smiles, making allowances, and takes a long drink. Then she kisses me, the first time in many weeks, and lets me suckle momentarily at the beer and lust on her tongue before she bats me away and hauls me through the bar by my belt loops, off to the bathroom.

She needn't have bothered pulling my pants up, as it turns out. Daddy pushes me into a stall, but doesn't lock or even shut the door. Pushing down my jeans and boxers, she bends me at the waist, shoves me forward over the toilet, and delivers thirty hard and fast smacks to my right asscheek. I hear encouraging groans of delight from behind me: more audience participation. Daddy loves being watched, and I feel her ratchet up her assault, although she remains silent. I, however, am not so restrained.

"Please, Daddy—please—I'm sorry," I wail. But there's no response until my right cheek is throbbing with as much fire as my left.

"Thought you were gonna pick up some tail, huh, little boy?" Daddy says, reaching around me to grab my dick. I don't answer, and Daddy doesn't seem to care. There's unzipping behind me and I feel the heavier weight of Daddy's bigger cock cool and firm against my ass. The pressure against my inflamed skin is enough to make me wince, but she doesn't stop at that. Daddy grinds into me, holding firmly to my dick so it rubs into my clit. The harder I push back against Daddy, into the hurt, the harder she works the base of my cock against my clit. But just as I get into it, panting and letting loose a groan, Daddy releases my silicone masturbator, yanks my hips up so my ass is level with her crotch, and slides her cock into my pussy. She slams home, driving the length of her dick so hard into me that I nearly scream.

"Yeah, Daddy knows how you like it," she says, and I groan

in agreement. Daddy pulls back sharply, and I shove backward to meet the thrust, almost losing my balance when it doesn't come. Daddy remains still. She rakes short fingernails across the tender skin of my ass, and I hiss in response.

"Did you miss me?"

"Yes, Daddy," I cry, hoping the desire in my voice turns her on enough that she'll just go on and fuck me.

"Was it worth it, your petulance and rudeness?"

In spite of the fat head of her dick holding my pussy open, and how good it feels to get fucked in this toilet stall, my resistance and stubbornness—pride—rises up like gorge. As if on cue, Daddy starts moving her cock, popping it up in short jerky thrusts so it shoves me open further and rubs against my G-spot. I flood with need and suddenly I don't care how it gets met.

"No, Daddy—it wasn't—I'm—sorry—" I gasp in between thrusts.

"Whose ass is this?" she grunts, having to hold herself back now.

"Yours, Daddy."

"And what do I do with it?" The thrusts get more erratic, going deeper until she remembers herself.

"Whatever you want, Daddy—whatever you want to do."

And with a sharp "That's right," Daddy plunges into me, yanking me backward so she slams into me. She fucks me quick and hard; the imprint of the tiles behind the toilet embeds itself into the palms of my hands. I can feel my belly and thighs begin to tense, but Daddy comes fast with a holler and slides out of my pussy with a soft pop.

"Clean yourself up—let's go get you off." By the time I stand, shaky and so heavy with need I can barely see, Daddy has left the stall. I wipe some of the wetness from my pussy and thighs and pull my pants back up. Leaving the bathroom, I move through scattered applause toward the cool night air coming through the open door. The cute bartender gives me an appreciative smile, one I'm unable to return; all of my attention is focused on maneuvering through the crowd without falling on my face.

I make it outside, and see Daddy at her car. My clit throbs in anticipation, and I manage to trot toward the door she's got open for me. But as I get closer, I find that there are other people in the car: Carly—and that bottom. Where in the hell did they find him on a Saturday night? Must have sent somebody trolling through the boy bars. I don't hesitate to climb into the backseat, though; my pussy insists. Daddy knows how to get me, and at least for now, I've no problem crouching at the feet of our guests. Right now, my ass would complain louder than my pride.

SMALL WINDOWS

Teresa Lamai

One

Josh always forces me to come right away.

He seeks out my cunt, stretched between chilly, immobilized thighs. He traces circles through the damp hair. His mouth is at my ear, whispering promises of torture, everything he's learned I despise, everything I need. His voice is soothing, drowsy. His other hand glides down my cheek, tests the pulse in my throat.

I don't know the difference between lust and fury anymore. My clit is swollen tight, my hips are shaking with rage. I can't move away but I try just the same. He laughs softly and kisses my navel. His tongue dips in and a clammy shiver moves through my stomach.

"Fuck you."

As soon as I say it, I know what's coming. I cringe behind the blindfold. He pulls the slap at the last second but still its impact makes my eyes burn.

My head rocks into the pillow. The camera flashes. He loves

to capture the fresh imprint of his palm, stark white in that instant before it marks crimson.

He slides two oiled fingers into my cunt and his thumb circles my clit until the come builds in my stomach, my feet, the crown of my head. The relentless sting becomes a low fire, sucking all my air, suffocating me.

But tonight he stops just before the orgasm breaks, lifting his hands away and giving my slick labia a swift, feathery kiss. I inhale to rail at him when I feel his teeth close hard over my clit. A starburst of silver and violet floods my vision.

"It's all right, Angela. Breathe more slowly."

It's several seconds before I feel anything but an icy rush. He takes off the blindfold and when I can see again, his palm is flat on my forehead, pressing my skull into the mattress. He forces a wedge of leather into my mouth, then reaches behind my head to fasten it there. His starched shirt has come untucked.

The pain crests and then ebbs to a dull, pounding ache. My clit throbs as if my heart has moved there.

And on the edges of the pain is a bliss so acute that my bones start to feel warm.

He kisses my cheeks. His eyes are grave, grateful. My shoulders are hitching with sobs. I try to writhe into his embrace.

"You don't want to stop," he murmurs. We both know it's not a question, but it could be.

I shake my head, thankful for the gag.

"You need it, Angie. You need it as badly as I do." He's trembling violently. He leans his forehead on mine. His sweat smells, sharply, of vinegar and blood. "Don't you, Angie? Tell me. Tell me 'yes.' "

I nod. My whole body aches for him.

"And do you want more, my beautiful girl, do you want even more? I know you do, but tell me."

I nod. My hands clench.

"God, you're beautiful." His voice breaks. I close my eyes. Soon, I know, he'll fall on the bed, his warm, clothed weight pressing gently at all of me. I go limp.

"Angie. Angie." He slaps my cheek, lightly. I open my eyes as a tight, quick curl of brightness disappears down my spine. "Listen to me. You'll lie here knowing that I'm coming back. Soon. Look at me. I want to give you both pain and tenderness—"

He stops, looking frightened, and kisses me. Then he's gone.

I watch the ceiling, trying not to move. This is a new torture, being left alone. His presence, his calm breath—those are the only things that make this bearable. I'm addicted to the need in his gaze. His face is radiant at times like this; he looks at me with something like love, but sharper, more visceral and pure.

The need in him is the mystery that keeps sucking at me. This compulsion frightens both of us, at times. But we keep feeding it, as if we expect that some day we'll just wake up calm and sated, free.

Fuck. I don't know when he turned the recorder on. He's left the monitor turned toward me. The last rays of sunset, pale apricot and scarlet, fall in stripes over the rumpled bed. My naked body is overexposed, gleaming sickly white in the blue-tinted screen. I don't recognize myself; my breasts are rounds of delicate mushroom flesh, my cunt a glistening, dark-furred maw. The screen is like an opening into a smaller, more vivid world, thick with black-green air, where an unfamiliar woman has let herself be drawn into view. He knew I'd be helpless to look away.

He used to tie me with yards and yards of rope, so that I lay almost swaddled, a live moth in a spider's web. In his first pictures of me, slivers of rosy tortured skin bulge through the nylon.

Now he keeps me down with only one or two fastenings. My wrists, cuffed and chained to the headboard. Some long metal bar attached to my ankles, keeping my legs far apart. My spine is stretched to its capacity, motionless. If I move my head it only makes me more aware of the dreadful gag. I feel my tongue swelling against the stubborn leather, and my clit heaves gently with the same movement.

Please come back. I hum it to myself from behind the gag. The sound echoes, trapped in my body. *Nothing is worse than being here without you, nothing.*

Two

I knew Josh by reputation before I met him. Our firm tried to recruit him two years ago, which gave me an excuse to introduce myself when he appeared at a conference in LA. I would have found some way to speak with him in any case. He was quietly, distantly handsome, his hair ash-blond, cat-tilted eyes full of dark, shifting colors—evergreen, blue, melancholy gray.

Most lawyers are desperately loud, calling out every word like a circus barker. Josh's serenity was strangely compelling; most feared he was vain, although he was unfailingly kind, almost self-effacing. When he first spoke to me, I felt a delicious calm.

"Angela." He said my name carefully, lowering his eyes as if he were trying to memorize it. His smile was intimate, just shy of inappropriate. I started to wonder if his diffidence covered a detached watchfulness—almost cruel in its acuity. "You seem like such a thoughtful woman. Powerful."

It was a ridiculous thing to say. I was, for once, speechless.

"It's strange to think that we've never met before," he continued. His eyes hadn't left mine. The hair at his temples glittered with silver.

"Well," I said brightly, looking past him, checking my watch.

Trying to salvage things. "It's good to...it's..."

He took my hand in his and squeezed it gently. Heat traveled to my shoulder. My breasts stung. I pulled my hand back and walked away.

I didn't recognize myself. I was a little alarmed.

He sat by me on the last day. There was a row of panel speakers, and I made a show of listening thoughtfully, typing gibberish into my laptop. My hands shook. I ducked out of the last presentation, afraid I'd make a fool of myself completely. I wandered about the lobby, pretending to take a phone call, shuffling some papers officiously through my folder.

I still don't know how he anticipated me, but when I ran for the elevator he was already inside. I let my eyes go blank, staring at our burnished, rippled reflections in the brass-plated doors. The old-fashioned buttons gleamed, one by one. If I didn't speak to him, I could take advantage of this small window of time to leave. Three more floors and this would all be over. I'd grab my suitcase, take a cab to the airport, catch an early flight.

I felt a cold draft at my back. Then my hair lifted slowly. I hadn't noticed the movement but his fingertips found my hair and were gliding through it, testing its weight and texture. The lightness of his touch was unbearable. I bit the inside of my cheek. Silvery threads of pleasure teased down my spine, spreading through my thighs.

I should have responded with outrage but after three or four heartbeats it was too late to do so plausibly. My eyes darted about. His fingertips grazed my scalp, the gentlest touch I'd ever felt. I didn't trust myself to speak. Two more floors.

Then his hand closed in my hair, pulling just a little, slowly. And something in me sprung open, cracked, burst, like a mechanical doll that had finally been wound too tight, too fucking tight. The soft pulling turned to pain. My hair was wrapped round his fist. I met his eyes then and he looked very serious, all smarmy artifice gone. *Fuck you*, I wanted to say. *Help me.* I was quiet.

My body knew this was what it had waited for, always. A muffled, outraged voice in my mind started shrieking at me. I swayed, softly. A stinging warmth washed through my stomach; my nipples burned like two tiny, brilliant points of light.

"In five minutes I'll be at your room," he explained. "You'll leave the door unlocked if you want me to come in. Be ready."

The doors hissed open and I was in the plush, gold-lit hallway.

I didn't know what "ready" meant. I decided it meant undressed, my hair pinned up, kneeling on the oatmeal-colored carpet. The room seemed very hot for a moment, then cold.

After thirty seconds of studious kneeling, I burst out laughing. I shook my head. "Oh, masterrr," I trilled up to the ceiling, then laughed some more. I rolled to my back, chuckling and snorting.

Honestly, a grown-ass woman, a bracing voice rang in my head. *You read too many goddamn novels. You need a hobby.*

I stood and picked up my stockings, still laughing so hard that a tear ran down my cheek. I covered my face, trying to take a deep breath. Then I sat, clutching my underwear, watching the unlocked door, laughing more quietly until just my stomach jittered, silently. I didn't move.

Seventeen minutes later I heard his measured footfalls outside. I slipped to the floor as the footsteps neared, slowed. When he opened the door my ragged breathing filled the room. I couldn't stop shaking.

He turned on the desk lamp as the door sucked itself closed. I cringed in the sudden light and glanced down at my breasts, lifting fitfully with each breath; the puffy, pale-violet nipples straining into the empty air. I felt small and lumpy without my clothes.

My pulse thudded through my stomach.

I ducked my head as he came near. My eyelids fluttered. He knelt at my back and I felt his quick breath as he pulled my elbows together and cinched my upper arms with his tie.

He sat opposite me. I watched his feet resting. My arms trembled with the effort of keeping still, but I didn't dare try to move them apart. If I kept perfectly still, I could almost pretend they weren't tied. Sweat rolled down between my shoulder blades.

"Angela, I want you to do what I say. I don't want you to speak unless I tell you to."

I wondered if he used that same delicately kind tone at work, on the street. A tone without supplication or threat, full of authority so natural it was unnoticed by the mind, but felt as deeply as sunlight.

I met his eyes then. I cast about in my mind for a long time, forcing my gaze to stay on his. "Why?" I said finally. My hair fell in my eyes and I tilted my head, blinking it out. I still hadn't let my arms even twitch.

I stood.

"I didn't tell you to stand, Angela. I didn't tell you to speak." His eyes lit up unmistakably, two phosphorescent points in the bland brown dimness. His glance traveled down my body. I fought down a moan as my cunt gripped itself.

I took a step back. My inner thighs kissed wetly and I blushed.

I willed my heart to beat more slowly, squinting in the gloom to find some sliding uncertainty in his smile, some twitch around his eyes that would show his disappointment. I felt as though I was backing into nothingness. His eyes were so still I couldn't look away. I wondered if it was sadness that weighted his gaze, kept it so steady.

"Do you want me to go, Angela?" His voice was tender. "I'll untie you and leave, I will. Just say that's what you want."

My heel crashed into a chair. I sank to a squat to catch my balance. My breasts slid against my knees. I tried to bring my arms forward but they were trapped. Panic spiked into my throat.

I saw his lips press together as I struggled instinctively, rising again.

"Kneel on the floor, Angela."

Now I couldn't stop struggling but the more I struggled the more I wanted to scream. "And if I don't?"

Fuck. Wrong response. His teeth flashed as he laughed, standing.

"Ah, you want to find out."

I backed away. As if I'd make a break for it, naked and half-tied. He reached me in two steps and his palm nudged into my breastbone. I shrieked, falling backward, my hands splayed desperately to break my fall.

My scream ended in a puff as I landed on the bed.

Before I could move again, he gripped my right thigh and folded my leg to my chest. His cheeks were flushed, but his breathing was still steady. My shoulders were burning, shocks of pain traveling to my neck. I tried to heave upward but his hand was like steel on my leg. His other hand rested softly over my cheek, brushing the hair from my eyes.

"You tell me, Angela, what should happen if you don't do what I ask?" His fingertips trailed down my throat. His mouth was a grim line but his eyes had a soft, avid gleam. His long lashes glinted in the lamplight.

My other foot rested on the bed. My cunt was lifted and stretched toward him, and before I could twist away he'd cupped his hand over the nest of damp curls. My labia swelled toward his fingertips. He watched my face. It was suddenly so hard to keep my eyes open.

"Tell me, Angela, tell me. Do you want me to hit you?" He

closed his eyes then, waiting for my answer.

Again something broke open in me, this time a series of small detonations along my spine. It felt as if I was there for five minutes, the blood rushing to my head, my cunt seething under the cool brush of his fingers. His touch was languid, innocent.

"You tell me, Angela."

"Yes."

I'd always thought that if I let a man tie me and hit me, I would let it happen only once, and I would never see him again. But when I saw how badly he needed it, the tiny shivers along his rigid arms, the small veins writhing in his temples, I didn't see how we could stop. I'll never forget the first time, the way he panted as he fastened my legs apart, the way he watched me struggle, his eyes entranced. I screamed when he finally entered me.

I have one cell phone just for his calls. When it vibrates, I drop everything. I feign sickness if I have to. I once left court and ran twenty blocks in the fog because there were no taxis. I thought my heart would burst.

Each time he opens the door the fugue starts again. I know once I see him I'll feel the shock in the solar plexus, the painful flash of heat behind my pubic bone that sears out all questions, that cauterizes my mind until it's closed and quiet. With Josh I'm a starfish, spread flat and writhing gently, mindless and swollen and tingling.

But come back. My eyes fly open and I sink my teeth into the gag. The wind lifts as the sky outside darkens. I strain to hear him in the front room. *Come back right now.*

Three

I jump when the door opens. Two shapes enter, one after another. I turn my head and squeeze my eyes shut.

"Angie, look." Josh's voice quiets me, even as I turn to stare at the girl.

I know her. The bed shifts gently when she sits. Her laugh is hot, sparkly.

She works in the café across the street from Josh's building, a shabby little box of music and chaotic colors. I've waited there more often that I'd ever admit, wondering when my cell phone would buzz.

"It *is* you," she smiles. I knew she was beautiful, her hair a glossy tumble of indigo black curls, her eyes enormous and startlingly dark, with long sleepy eyelids.

She's always flirted with me, although I've made a point of not speaking to her. I usually sit at a stool, alone, and she eventually finds an excuse to sit beside me, smirking and sleek, turning her head quickly and trying to meet my eyes.

"Is your deal that you don't talk to strangers, ever? Or just girls in cafés?" She doesn't even take her boots off as she reclines beside me. She's still cool from the evening wind and goose bumps ripple over my waist.

But her eyes are distracted, over her feral smile. She keeps glancing toward Josh. She whispers him a plaintive question, one that I can't hear over the roaring in my head. His refusal is curt.

She turns to me and stares at my gag. I roll my head away when her fingertips rest on my stretched lips. Her hand fits over my cheekbone, pulling my face back toward hers.

"Josh, do you always gag her like this? I couldn't take it."

When she raises herself on one elbow, I can see the monitor again. The gag's straps are cutting welts into my cheeks. I look like a bloated white snake next to her tiny form. Her heart-shaped bum is writhing slowly, a lush swell under soft black leather.

"Do you like this gag?" She kisses my temple and her hair slides across my face, pooling over my eyelids. My head fills with her scent, honey and cloves. I bite into the leather, my tongue fighting miserably for space.

"Ah, don't suck on it, you'll just make it worse." She pushes on it delicately. She glances toward Josh and he gives a soft noise of approval.

"Do you want it out? I asked you." Her eyes are close to mine. She tickles along my jaw. Her fingernails are sharp in my neck. I nod once.

"I'll take it out." She sits up. The monitor flashes behind her and I can't see her face in the dark. Just her eyes glittering dully.

"I'll take it out after you come."

She smiles with all her small kitten teeth, crouches between my knees. The tops of her dark breasts swell out of her camisole top, nuzzling each other softly. Holding my gaze, she places her thumbs along my labia and spreads me open. Her eyes widen.

I jump when the flash hits. Josh is standing over the bed now, the Polaroid exploding again and again. The photo cards drop to the floor. After five, he lets the camera fall near my head and gathers the photos.

The girl parts the hair from the top of my mound, where the labia cleave. Josh crosses to the window and throws the photos out into the dusk.

Her pinkies are at my anus and she giggles when I flinch. She lets them stray close to my cunt, almost close enough for me to snatch them in.

She fits her mouth over my clit, nursing intently, her beautiful head turned to the side, her long lashes resting on her cheeks. Her dark skin shimmers with ruby glints. Two strong fingers slide into me and I start bucking. My thighs are tingling; a rush of sweet yearning fills me. I lift my hips and she presses hard, her mouth a burning center for both of us.

My back snaps straight. Pleasure flashes along my spine,

twisting and writhing like a chemical fire, full of strange colors, uncontrollable and fearsome. I can't stop writhing against her sweet, sweet mouth. The camera flashes again, again, again.

I'm still coming when she moves up my body. Her chin is glistening, her mouth smeared with wine-colored lipstick. As she rests her cheek on mine, my own scent, a cloying musk of merlot and crushed flowers, fills my head.

"Well done, Angela." I feel her fumbling for the buckle at the base of my skull. "Well done. And now I want this gag off you so we can hear you scream."

Fear prickles over my skin, making my body tighten again. When the gag comes out all I can do is gulp the cool air and lick my lips, closing my eyes to breathe deep. Her slim thighs straddle my hips. She holds a thin cane, glowing ivory. She rests her forefingers on either end of it, balancing it delicately as if it were a violin bow.

The room is dark now, thick with turquoise-blue night air. The only light is the flickering of the monitor and the distant topaz glow of the streetlight. Josh is walking toward us.

"Will you let me watch this film later?" She wets one thumb and brushes it over my right nipple, making small crosses, her touch light as a moth wing. She catches my gaze and flicks her wrist, snapping the cane to the underside of my breast. She clamps her legs around me when I buck. Her wild hair bounces.

The pain spreads through my rib cage. Warming. I look at Josh and hear myself saying, "Again. Please."

I feel the bar being removed from my feet, then my body being turned over, my wrists still fastened. The cane taps lightly on my ass, then slides down one thigh. Josh stretches out beside me. He pushes one hand under my pubic bone and lets me fit my fat, aching mound into his palm. My clit is like a tiny bird struggling to fly.

His shuddering voice is so close at my ear, his tongue tracing along the ridged skin between words. "Which do you want more, Angela, the cruelties or the tenderness?"

"Both," I whisper, and his other hand traces the back of my neck.

When he kisses my cheek, pain flashes over my right buttock. I wonder if she's split the skin. I gasp for air. My cunt sucks at Josh's fingers and I'm dizzy as if I've been caught in the churning center of a wave.

SILENCE IS GOLDEN

Rachel Kramer Bussel

SILENCE IS GOLDEN read the sign on Dean's bedroom wall. The statement struck me as odd the first time I saw it, and every time thereafter. Dean is a therapist, after all, paid to listen to people talking all day and often into the night. But I quickly learned that for him, silence isn't just golden, it's paramount.

"You talk too much," he told me on our first date. I chose to take that as a compliment, babbling away even more after he'd uttered the words, even though I knew he meant he wanted me to shut up. I picked at my fries, my burger open and messy, rare red meat staring back at me as my gaze flitted from my unfinished dinner up to his pale blue serious eyes. The more solemn and serious he looked, the brattier I wanted to be, so I poured about a quarter of the ketchup bottle onto my plate, drowning each fry in a sea of red. He was so silent I wound up spilling my secrets, talking and eating, eating and talking, undone by his intense stare, not sure what he thought of my antics. His eyes took in everything; he seemed to be looking right through me, even as

I poured out my heart, secrets, fantasies and all.

This was our first *date* date, but we'd been chatting online for a month. "Chat" is such a tame word for what we were doing. "Fucking each other's brains out" would've been more accurate. Even though we had sex virtually, our encounters were still real as anything to me; he made me wetter than I could ever remember being. That first week, anyway, it was suck, fuck, cock, pussy, lick, bite, tease. But then the requests became more demanding, and just the sight of his screen name, *SirDean*, simple and direct, made me so horny I couldn't do anything but slam my fingers inside myself, hopelessly trying to fill myself up as he kept up his stream of filthy, flirty talk. I'd toss my bags onto the floor in the hallway as soon as I got home, not caring if my roommates tripped over them, shoving the door back with my heel as I raced to my computer, surrendering to the screen. "Do you have a dildo?" he'd asked during that first week. I'd told him I did, and he made me tell him exactly how I fucked myself. Soon thereafter, he told me how long and how often I could use it, making me wait to jerk off for days at a time.

When we finally met in person, I hadn't come in three days and was dripping onto the leather seat beneath me. I was nervous, excited, aroused and overwhelmed, all at once, and my natural reaction was to talk. I told him about flashing my neighbors with my white cotton underwear when I was a bratty teenager; about the first guy who fingered me, in a movie theater; told him about the job I'd left on a lunch break and never returned to. I let it all pour out over my uneaten, soggy burger, sitting there surrounded by a sea of soggy fries and sloppy red sauce. I was still going when he took one of his big, ink-stained fingers and held it up to my lips.

"I think you just haven't met the person who'll shut that sweet little mouth. You have better things to do with it than talk." As he said that, he lifted my foot out of my shoe and held it against his hard cock under the table. He rubbed it against his erection, but only when I was silent. If I talked, he moved my foot to the side. It was a childish way to reinforce his point, but it worked, and I squelched my urge to tell him every thought racing through my head. When I started to open my mouth to do anything other than eat, he'd squeeze my foot in a way that almost hurt but mostly sent shooting stars of arousal right to my pussy.

Back at his place, my natural garrulousness kicked in again and I couldn't help whispering in his ear. "You make me so wet," I told him, because it was true. He did, even when I wasn't with him—just thinking about him had my pussy halfway to the moon. But he didn't respond as I'd have expected, as every other guy I'd told the same thing to had. No, instead of pushing me down and pressing his cock against me, he shoved his fingers inside me. Two in my mouth and two in my cunt. I moaned against his hand.

"What does the fucking sign say, Jill? *Silence is golden.* I'm going to have to gag you; that's the only way to make you shut up, clearly." His voice was tight, and I couldn't tell if he was really annoyed or not. Even though his fingers inside my cunt had paused, I was still aching for him. I shut my eyes and vowed to be quiet. His fingers were starting to pinch my lips, but I swallowed the noise that threatened to rise up, spreading my legs further even as my panties cut into my legs, the elastic warring with my need to be wide open for him.

He slowly released his grasp and shoved me onto my back on his bed, then walked away. My arms automatically went over my head and my pussy tightened instantly when I saw him return with a coil of rope and a gag, its bright red ball attached to leather straps stirring something primal inside me. I'd never been gagged before, at least not formally. I'd had plenty of things shoved in my mouth, though: fingers, a cock, my own wet panties, and every time I'd practically creamed myself. The sound of my muffled moans, the reverberations through my body, knowing that someone cared enough to actually make me be quiet instead of just admonishing me, all got me so wet I almost couldn't stand it.

I wanted to please him, so I opened my mouth wide, staring at him, begging for it, while my hands remained above my head. "Good girl," he said, patting my long hair once before he moved behind me and fastened the gag. It fit right there in my mouth, and he buckled it against the back of my head, leaving me feeling more vulnerable than I ever had before. This was new for me. I'd have to speak with my eyes, with my body, with my energy. He let the end of the rope trail against my armpit and I flinched, and then he did it again, tickling me as I tried to maintain my composure. I must've done all right, because he laced my wrists together with the thick white rope, then fastened them to the headboard so that I was lying on my back in the middle of his bed. I still had my clothes on, but not for long.

He pulled down my skirt first, easily removing the short garment, followed by my panties—the pretty pink silk ones I'd carefully chosen, only to realize now that they didn't really matter; the thin fabric was soaked by the time he pulled it off. "Mmmm," I moaned against the gag. I squirmed when he dove between my legs, his tongue lightly lapping at me, teasing me. He wasn't ready to let me come, not yet. His tongue went away the minute I really started to enjoy it; as soon as I began to buck back against him, raising my hips, straining against the rope, he stopped.

"Not just yet, my sweet." He unzipped his pants and showed me the cock I'd only seen in photos. This time I moaned because I wanted it in my mouth so badly. I gave him a pleading look, and he sank down so his legs straddled me, then moved closer so he could jerk off right in my face. I watched close-up as his fist molded to his cock, slowly pumping it before he shifted to glide the tip against my cheek. "Don't worry, Jill, I know how much you want my cock buried inside your throat. There'll be plenty of time for that. You look so beautiful right now. I want to teach you to be quiet so that later I can hear you scream," he said, tapping his dick against my cheek. My pussy was so tight by then I could barely take in his words.

He made me wait, and I really had no choice. Oh, we'd worked out a code, a way I could thump my leg on the mattress if I needed to get loose, but it wasn't a matter of safety. It was pure lust, the kind that makes you willing to do anything to be close to the person who's driving you mad. Anything—like posting your naked photo on a message board, or flying across the country to meet the man who's tormented you even in your dreams. It was an impractical affair, but my pussy wouldn't listen, and that's how I wound up fervently praying for him to finally fuck me.

First, he made sure to kiss and lick and tease and tickle every inch of my splayed-out body. By the time he was ready to fuck me, I'd actually lost the impulse to speak; all my energy was focused on my cunt. When he slid into me, I stared up at him with wide, needy eyes, and he read me perfectly. He knew he had me stretched out in every way possible, my arms straining, my mouth filled, my pussy just waiting for him, and when he saw fit to fill me up, he rammed his thick, hard pole into me, hitting my sweetest spots.

I shut my eyes then and listened to the near silence, the only sounds in the room his soft moans and the slippery sound of him entering me, my wetness speaking for me. I realized his wisdom the more aroused I got, my usual grunts and groans sliding back down my throat to be swallowed and consumed as I opened wider and wider.

The thousands of messages we'd sent to each other in a short span of time boiled down to this moment, and I made sure to listen, and to feel every thrust. He sensed when I switched over, when I shifted from earth girl, bound and gagged, to somewhere else in the universe, a hungry hole, a woman out of this world, ready for anything. He gave me all of himself and then some, taking me apart so I could see myself anew. The silence rang in my ears as I came, the absence of sound coaxing me over the edge as my saliva pooled in my mouth, my burning wrists took in the imprints of the rope, and I reveled in his fast, hard, hammering thrusts. When we were done, there was no need to speak.

He silently removed my bonds and I buried my head in his sweaty chest, too spent for anything more than listening to his heartbeat, the only sound in the room I wanted to hear.

THE '76 REVOLUTION

Nikki Magennis

Nineteen-seventy-six hit me like a supernova. Turned me inside out. Punk was breaking out all over the country. Glasgow, with its bleak concrete and razor gangs, with the ever-simmering rage of a downtrodden city, joined in like the drunk guy at a party. At least, a handful of angst-ridden teenagers joined in. I thought it was the best chance to dress up I'd ever had. A fashion student in the seventies—what would you expect?—overnight I ditched my feathered bangs and dyed everything black, to the shock of my boyfriend. Ripped up my clothes, stitched them back together with some artfully placed safety pins, and left the house as a newly fledged punkette.

I strutted into the student union in my new gear, and I could feel his eyes fixed on me as I crossed the room.

"Rosie?"

"Hey Steve," I said, playing it cool.

"What the fuck?" He picked up a strand of my newly jet-black hair, and lifted it like he was weighing his options.

"Like it?"

"But your hair was so pretty..."

I knew how much he loved my hair. When we were having sex, he'd bury his face in it and moan. Always loved to touch things, Steve. He was a sculptor, a couple of years older than me. Worked in clay and soapstone. He'd run his hands over my body and murmur how soft I felt.

Everything was smooth and soft and beautiful with Steve, right down to his shaggy Afghan coat and his hippy ideals.

I shrugged.

"Time for a change."

I'd never used the word *love* with Steve—even though I was young and reckless. I didn't want to be tied to anyone or anything. Even so, my heart hurt a little as I left him in the union and headed for the city center.

I turned heads as I walked down Sauchiehall Street. People stared, some even swore at me. I stuck my chin in the air and kept walking, breathing in the sharp air of the future. I was going to jump headfirst into the New Wave—even if I had to do it alone.

Downtown, I ran the gauntlet of dingy record shops, rifling through the homemade record sleeves with my hands in fingerless lace mittens.

Back home in my apartment I played screeching, earsplitting songs that lasted two minutes if I was lucky. I got a crush on Patti Smith, and played *Horses* over and over. It felt like I'd discovered a new religion.

But it wasn't only Steve who hated the new brutalism. The godfearing masses of suburbia choked on their tea when the Pistols first said "shit" on live television. Within a couple of months there was a backlash.

The city fathers banned punk. The music, the clothes, the attitude were all too much for them to handle. Me in my polka-dot dresses and bondage boots, heavy kohl round my innocent blue eyes—*I* was banned. And delighted. How illicit and how cool to have to travel out of town to the nearest underground club, where I could pogo to the Buzzcocks and drink cider and blackcurrant till I was sick.

A rain-soaked Friday night, and the coach was filling with rebels and vagabonds. I was tarted up in my best distressed gear—hair crimped and sneer firmly in place. I'd perfected a way of looking out through my fringe that I was sure smacked of spite and cool fuck-you attitude.

The steps onto the bus were a problem—I was hobbled in a skirt with ripped straps that constrained my legs, making large strides impossible. I could totter down Sauchiehall Street like a geisha, but climbing stairs was tricky, without the whole ridiculous shebang riding up my thighs and exposing my ripped fishnets to the guys queuing behind me.

"That skirt should be illegal."

I twisted round and saw a guy in a white shirt and jeans. It was Steve, looking up at me with that kind of smooth, stoned smile he had that made him look like a Buddhist monk.

"Fuck off," I said, into my hair, then climbed up into the bus and strode toward the back, nodding at Ange and Jo and Kris, all my fellow dropouts on their way to the freak show. I got a thrill out of shocking people. Loved it, in fact. It felt like a little victory to elicit insults from strangers, and in my head I'd reclassified Steve as someone I didn't know.

I dropped into a seat, and shook the rain out of my hair, deliberately not looking at anyone. But it was my turn to be shocked. Steve had followed me onto the bus.

"Hey Rosebud," he said, looking down at me with that cool, dark smile. "Where you going?"

"The Silver Thread. Why do you want to know?"

"Because I'd follow that sweet little ass of yours to the ends of the earth, baby."

This was unexpected. I'd got more used to attracting catcalls than chat-up lines. I didn't quite know what to do. He swung down to sit next to me.

"You make that outfit yourself?"

I fixed him with a steely eye and nodded once.

"I like it. Specially the tights…" His gaze waltzed down my body and ran along my legs, lingering where the rips in my fishnets exposed the smooth white skin of my thighs. I had to fight the urge to tug my frayed-hem miniskirt down further. I was cool; I didn't care if I showed too much flesh.

"Since when are you into fashion?" I said, trying to keep the bravado harsh in my voice.

He merely reached out to lift a tendril of rain-wet hair from my face, twisting it round his finger.

"Since I saw it wrapped round the beautiful body of a girl I once knew," he said. I couldn't help it, a definite glimmer of a turn-on started as he wound my hair round his fingertip and tugged gently. He looked at me with dark eyes. The coach engine rattled into gear. Steve let go and jumped to his feet.

"When do you get back?"

"Two."

I didn't think he'd be there. Not at that hour, not after I'd been so rude to him. But then, at that point I didn't know just how intense Steve was. In his mind we were entangled, fated to meet again.

I fell asleep on the bus home, tired and half-drunk, ears ringing from hours of loud music. Woke up to the sound of the brakes, the driver shouting at us to get off. I stumbled out onto the street, still dizzy with the edge of a sharp cider-hangover cutting into my thoughts. And there he was, leaning against the wall at the exact spot where I'd left him. Giving me his Zenlike smile. Careful to hide it behind my hair, I smiled back.

He walked me home through empty streets, walking with an easy pace, not saying much. The rain had stopped, and the city was washed clean, silvered and quiet. We slipped into the house, and I showed him into my room. A dressmaker's dummy stood in the center, draped in ribbon and strips of cloth. Pincushions, scissors, and cut-up dresses littered the floor.

"How's the dressmaking?" he asked, lifting a roll of lace and letting it play through his hands, feeling the texture against his skin.

"I'm a designer, Steve," I said. "You know, like Vivienne Westwood. Those are some of my new pieces," I told him, nodding at the dress rail. Net and lace and sequins spilled from every hanger—outlandish clothes, but carefully made.

"Wow. How do you get your ideas?"

I shrugged. "You know, I just play around. Try stuff out on the mannequin. Rip it apart, tie it back on. Fuck it up, make it unique."

"Sounds like fun."

He approached me, the roll of lace in his hand and a dark fire in his eyes.

"Let me try something?"

"What are you suggesting?"

"I'm suggesting we play around, baby. Close your eyes."

He waited. "Come on. Trust me."

He wound a strip of lace over my eyes, knotting it tightly behind my head so it wouldn't slip. I felt his hands trail down, run through my hair to the tips. Then he was holding my hands and pulling them gently behind me, winding more lace around my wrists. Binding me.

"Wait, Steve, I—"

He shushed me, putting a finger to my lips.

"Just relax. You're going to love this."

He was unzipping my dress, pulling it free. I couldn't see what was going on, but I could feel every brush of his hand against me, the dress pulling downward as it came off, the sudden cold of the air in the room as it hit my skin.

Then I was standing in my underwear, and my room was suddenly a foreign country, electric with suspense. Steve moved away, I heard his steps move around the room. And then I felt his mouth next to my ear, his hot breath on my neck.

"Don't move a muscle, Rosebud. That's very important, okay?"

I nodded assent, but it still made me jump when I felt the cold steel against my chest—the flat of the scissors touching me as Steve cut my bra away. That wicked little snipping sound as he worked down, the steady rasp of the scissors shredding my tights, my panties. I couldn't stop myself from crying out—I was more than a little bewildered.

When he'd finished, my tits and pussy were bared, my clothes hanging off me in shreds. I thought then that he was ready to start. I was almost ready to beg for it.

But I hadn't quite understood.

He bound me with the roll of lace, winding it round my torso, across my breasts, leaving the nipples bare but digging into the soft flesh so I could feel the pattern pressing against me. He kept winding, round my hips and between my legs, pulling the lace tight so that it rubbed deliciously against my pussy. He wound it round my legs, binding them tight so I swayed to keep my balance, then knotted it tightly round my ankles.

"Now that's what I call an outfit," he said, a slight shake in his voice giving him away. "Want to see how you look?"

I nodded, unable to speak.

When he took the blindfold off, I was facing the full-length mirror. For the first time ever, I shocked myself. I'd never seen anything more lewd, more horny. I was wrapped so tight that the ribbon cut into my flesh and spilled over it, and my modest little breasts were squeezed upward so that they seemed juicier than ever. Between the lace, my clit protruded, and a shine of moisture on my thigh betrayed just how wet I was.

"Like it?"

"Yes."

"You inspired me. Bend over."

I was a moment too slow to obey his command. Steve put his hand on the small of my back and gently tipped me forward, holding tight on to my hips to stop me from falling. Trussed like this, I was at his mercy, and the knowledge thrilled me as much as the feeling of lace tight against my skin.

He traced the ribbon across my body, letting it lead his hand between my legs, where he lingered. When his finger swept over my slit and burrowed into my hole, I felt my knees buckle. I couldn't fall, though, because he was holding me up. Keeping my ass high enough to get his cock inside me, running it into me like a knife into butter. Bent over like that, I felt the thrust of his cock deeper than ever before—it was a very thorough fucking I got. Not the smooth sex we'd had before; this time it was darker. Darker and more intense. Steve was using the lace as some kind of harness, restraining me so he could fuck me however he pleased. Pushing his cock into me with long, maddeningly slow strokes. The more I squirmed in my lace bonds, trying to speed up the rhythm, the tighter the knots became and the firmer Steve held me. I could barely move, only open my mouth to beg him—"Please, Steve."

"Please what, Rosebud? You want to come? Huh?"

"Yes. Yes, I want to come. Please."

He reached round to tug on the lace, the strand that ran between my legs and chafed against my clit. It burned, burned so good. I was writhing and bucking then, trying to increase the friction and work my way to a climax.

But only when *he* was ready, only when his cock twitched and stiffened inside me and I knew he was going to come, only then did he tug hard enough to tip me over the edge. He fucked me with a few hard, decisive strokes and I felt the buzzing and streaming of his cock inside me just as I hit meltdown myself.

It was such a release, that orgasm, I could have fallen face-first onto the floor, crashed across the dress rail and screamed myself hoarse. But Steve held on to me tighter than ever as I came, keeping me steady so all the movement happened inside me, the screaming and the crashing were inside my cunt, transforming into hard spasms of pleasure that left me open-mouthed and gasping.

Afterward he loosened the knots so gently, so carefully. He rubbed my skin to get the circulation going. Wrapped me in a quilt he picked up from the floor, and kissed me, finally, on the lips. "Okay?"

I nodded dumbly. We sat facing each other on my bed, dawn turning the sky pale. My wrists still bore red marks from the lace, and I touched them gently, feeling the ache, the slight sting from where the lace had pressed into me. Even after he'd undone my bindings, I still felt tied. Wonderfully tied, for the first time ever.

BOUND TO KILL

Lisette Ashton

Pain came with the first slice. The cane snapped smartly across her bare bottom and Linda squealed. A red-hot wire of agony blazed across both cheeks. Instantaneously, the heat tightened into a warm, fluid rush that filled her sex. The combination of humiliation and arousal was sickeningly exciting. Linda blushed, cringed, and then waited to discover what would happen next.

"Craig Logan's name wasn't on this month's hit list," Miss Burroughs growled.

She slashed the cane down again and this time Linda howled. The woman had a gift for accuracy and landed the second blow directly across the path that had been laid by the first. The blaze of pain burnt with greater intensity before transforming into a reminder of the same diabolical heat that already smoldered within Linda's sex. Her pussy lips glistened with the warmth of fresh sweat and her inner muscles trembled as though she was on the verge of shuddering through a climax.

"You were employed to terminate the contact," Miss Burroughs complained. "And we invested a lot of time and effort in getting you into the right place, with the right information, at the right time."

"I know," Linda moaned.

The cane slashed down for a third time and Linda held herself rigid for fear of collapsing from either pain or pleasure. She teetered on the brink of being overwhelmed by both responses and couldn't guess which was likely to win.

"Our agents spent months researching the contact's habits, lifestyle, and social and business circles, and you knew he was to be terminated," Miss Boroughs hissed. "You understood the remit for your contract: yet you failed."

The fourth blow wrought an orgasm. Biting across the same aching line of flesh that was already crimson from repeated punishment, it sired a scorching heat that went beyond unbearable.

Linda wailed. Echoes of bitter pleasure flooded through her. With an undignified roar, she vented her cry in a blend of euphoria and anguish.

"Why did you fail, Linda? Why?"

Lying on the floor, sobbing from a meld of distress and delight, Linda couldn't bring herself to answer. All she could do was remember the fatal error that had brought her to meet Miss Burroughs; displeasure.

The lifestyle of a professional assassin was everything Linda had hoped. She attended glamorous cocktail parties, possessed a host of James Bond-esque gadgets and traveled the world at someone else's expense. Her employers used businesslike euphemisms to cloud their conversations with respectability—*contract*, instead of instructions to kill; *hit list*, to describe the monthly record of those who had been executed; *contact*, instead of victim; and *terminate* rather than murder—and the morality of her actions seldom crossed her mind. Whenever Linda did consider what she was doing, she congratulated herself on being one of those fortunate enough to financially benefit from the whole, horrible world of hired assassins.

As in the case of Craig Logan, a philandering husband and treacherous employee whose wife and bosses had pooled resources to have him terminated. Research had uncovered that his life insurance was pitifully lapsed, and Linda had read the signed declaration that said his employers were not going to gain from his death. The only ones who would financially profit from Craig's termination were Linda and her employers.

Miss Burroughs had thoughtfully provided a detailed file on the contact's tastes and, as a consequence, Linda had bleached her hair and transformed her locks into the shade of blonde Craig favored in his women. She also purchased a designer outfit that combined those styles and colors that had caught his interest in the past, then placed herself in the hotel bar he was scheduled to frequent.

Getting him there had been a simple matter of his employers summoning him to meet a fictitious client. Linda idly flirted with Craig as he waited for a man who was never going to arrive.

And their chatter turned to sexual banter, Linda enjoying Craig's playful lechery and encouraging him to become bolder. Knowing his predilections, having read the entire dossier on the contact's likes and dislikes, she waited until he made a second reference to the suite at his disposal before demurely shaking her head. "I don't think you'd enjoy the sort of games I play in hotel bedrooms," she confessed. Lowering her voice, making sure that none of the other guests in the bar could hear, she whispered, "I like bondage."

They were three words that had him exactly where she wanted-ed. From that moment she knew her contract was as good as complete and Craig Logan was all but terminated.

Admittedly, they stayed in the bar for another drink, Craig teasing her with talk of how they could play and what they could do for each other, but they might as well have been in the bedroom. Casual caresses progressed to the curious, then urgent, touches of the sexually inquisitive. His leg stroked her inner thigh, she traced her fingers over the back of his hand, and he sensually stroked her cheek when she graced him with a coy blush. Miss Burroughs had once told Linda that there was no aphrodisiac greater than the knowledge that you had the power of life and death in your hands but, after meeting Craig, Linda was ready to argue that opinion. There was a greater aphrodisiac: the satisfaction of wanting someone and knowing they wanted you with the same anxious passion.

And, when they stumbled into his suite an hour later, she learned there were other stimulants for her libido that she had never previously discovered, from the hot, hungry kisses he planted against her mouth and neck, to the subtle stimulation of being caressed through her clothes. The delights of binding a naked man were something she had tried previously but they had never excited her as powerfully as with Craig. Their conversation in the bar had indicated how he wanted to be treated and she was won over by the rush of sensuality his suggestions provoked. Standing above him on the bed after slowly removing her stockings, she taunted him with their silky caress as the sheer hosiery stroked across his bare skin. He writhed beneath the teasing, gritting his teeth and grinning like a lunatic. With one breath he was begging her to take him and then, with the next, he was pleading that she should make him wait. After prolonging his agony as much as she dared, and stroking the second stocking around his erection until he almost came, Linda deigned to secure his wrists. She bound his ankles with a pair of ties from his open suitcase and then continued to torment him with kisses and caresses that had him cursing bitterly.

His erection looked unbearably hard, a pain that clearly worsened when she raised the hem of her skirt and forced the sodden gusset of her panties over his nose. Her cleft was already sopping with need and she knew the crotch of her underwear held the scent of musk.

Craig bucked and cursed and thrashed beneath her. His agonized complaints reminded her briefly of those messier contacts she had terminated, when her victims went through their pitiful, reluctant death throes. She didn't know if Craig would ultimately fall into that category and, with her mind concentrating on the task at hand, she didn't bother speculating on a subject so unpleasant. Fretful that she might give something away if she turned her thoughts in that direction, Linda reminded herself that she was supposedly a professional and tried to concentrate on teasing the contact. It didn't promise to be too great a challenge because his tongue was working delicious miracles against the sodden fabric that covered her cleft.

The fear of discovery never troubled Linda. She was staying at the hotel under an assumed identity, the blonde hair would become raven black in the morning and there were no records of her fingerprints on any of the world's databases. Even though she was leaving a trail of CCTV footage and DNA samples for subsequent investigators, Linda knew that she would remain safe from capture and prosecution once she had completed this contract.

Freed by the liberating lack of consequences, she used Craig with a lust that almost matched his ferocity. Gingerly, she eased the fabric of her panties aside and allowed him to taste the fresh, unfettered flesh of her labia. His warm kisses slipped wetly against the folds of her pussy lips and she was almost choked by her body's mounting need for orgasm. She could see his thickness never waned—he remained perpetually hard as he lapped at her—and the idea that he was so excited by his bound submission added volume to Linda's enjoyment.

When she finally pulled her pussy from his face, then pushed her sopping sex lips over his length, she knew he was battling to stave off his release. Determinedly trying to wring the climax from him, squeezing her muscles and sliding up and down, she was amazed that he could resist the impulse to come.

The idea of concluding the contract crossed her mind, but she wanted to see if Craig was really as proficient a lover as she suspected. Scratching her nails down his chest, biting one of his nipples while she continued to rise up and down on his shaft, Linda listened to his faux pleas for mercy as she tried to push him beyond the brink of self-restraint.

His climax only came when she leaned back on her haunches, splayed the folds of her pussy and, with his shaft still quivering inside her hole, teased herself to climax. Her fingertips were slippery with the wetness of sweat and mingled sex secretions, her clit felt inordinately sensitive, and the rush of joy came quick and with unseemly haste. Linda's paroxysms of pleasure brought Craig to orgasm and his length pulsed deep inside her sex. She climbed from his bound body with a groan of satisfaction.

"My turn," he sighed.

Without considering what she was doing Linda agreed.

She allowed him to tie her hands above her head and savored the sensuous touch of his fingers as he made sure her bonds were inescapable. It crossed her mind that she was putting herself in an invidious position, the brief fear of treachery pinched her nerves, and she worried that he might want to do more than merely pleasure her. But, once she had put those disquieting distractions aside, Linda found she was reveling on a new plateau of bliss.

It was amazing to think that she had never encountered such a gifted lover. He worked his tongue into the folds of her sex, tormenting her clitoris until she was on the brink of orgasm, before darting away to leave her frustrated and begging him for more. His first orgasm had left his shaft limp, but the more he kissed her bare breasts and intimate crevices the harder he became. By the time he was positioning himself between her legs, she knew he was more than rigid enough to satisfy her needs. When he began to ride her, she wondered why she had never been fortunate enough to meet a man like Craig Logan before.

The majority of her contracts involved sex before the termination—she was an attractive young woman and it was only sensible to use that advantage to put her targets in a vulnerable position—but no element of her work had prepared Linda for the thrill of being bound and used by such a gifted expert. Craig was innovative and exciting. He timed his thrusts so that she grew used to the rhythm and then unsettled her by an unexpected change in pace. At first, he plowed briskly between her legs, his shaft hammering frantically in and out. Then he paused— pushed himself deep inside—then withdrew with a lazy, languid ease that took his tip to the brink of slipping from her pussy.

She struggled with the bindings at her wrists; anxious to break free, take him in her embrace and make him force her past the peak of climax. Aside from the glorious wetness that now lathered her inner thighs, her cheeks had become daubed with tears of frustration. Every muscle in her restrained body ached with the need to orgasm, and she sobbed and begged for him to make her come.

Obligingly, Craig pushed deep into her sex and let his second climax carry her to a new realm of satisfaction. Waves of bliss and sweet sensuous delight overwhelmed Linda and had her screaming gratefully into the night. When he placed his mouth

over hers, she didn't know if he was trying to mute her exclamations, or merely savor the full benefits of her release.

He untied her hands, and they continued to kiss until both
fell wearily onto the bed. Suddenly saddened by her reason for
being there, and trying to salvage a little professional pride after
the indignity of giving herself to him so wholeheartedly, Linda
pushed Craig back to the bed and straddled his bare body.

He made no protest when she refastened the bindings at his
wrists and ankles, and his erection eventually twitched back to
life once she had started to lick the remnants of their shared wetness from his shaft. Common sense told her that she ought to
complete the contract, and terminate him before there was any
risk of discovery, but Linda knew she would always regret the
action if she didn't allow herself to experience Craig Logan for
one final time.

"So tell me, Linda," Miss Burroughs repeated, "why isn't he on
the hit list?"

The woman towered over her, still wielding the cane and
looking more than ready to use it again. Linda didn't know if
that thought brought feelings of despair or hope. She struggled to
get back on her knees again, displaying her bare bottom to suffer
more of her superior's brutal discipline. Her legs felt weak and
she was in danger of trembling from the exertion of the orgasm.

Miss Burroughs raised her cane high. "Why didn't you terminate your contact, Linda? Why?"

"I couldn't," Linda gasped.

She expected to feel another slice from the cane, but this time
Miss Burroughs refrained from delivering the punishment. There
was a deathly pause, a silence like concrete wedged between
them, and then the woman lowered her cane. "You couldn't?
What stopped you?"

"I stopped me," Linda said honestly. She was struggling to find words to explain her actions but, with the rush of arousal still coursing through her body, it was difficult to articulate her reply. "I stopped me for the good of humanity."

"What do you mean by that?"

Linda drew a deep breath and decided she could only give an honest answer. Staring meekly up at her superior, knowing the answer was going to meet with the sternest censure but no longer fearing the consequences, she said, "I didn't terminate him because I thought a man who fucks that good doesn't deserve to die."

And, although the subsequent caning transcended the unbearable, Linda was surprised to discover that Miss Burroughs didn't take the disciplinary procedure any further. Afterward, Linda discovered that her superior had generously volunteered to go out into the field and take care of the same contact. But, and this was the thing that always puzzled her, Craig Logan's name never appeared on Linda's copy of the hit list.

BURY IT, OFFICER

Ryan Field

By the time I pulled off the interstate and into the rest area, the rain had stopped, leaving the black road slick and shiny with a smell of wet grass in the air. As I slowly circled the parking lot, carefully checking out the truck area, I realized it was an empty night. One other car—a black sedan—and not a trucker in sight. Already two in the morning and I didn't want to cruise all night, so I parked about two spaces away from the black sedan, killed the engine of my black SUV, and turned off the headlights. Though the windows were darkly tinted and dotted with rain and I couldn't see very well, the guy sitting in the black sedan seemed fairly young and surprisingly attractive. Driving an SUV and being so high up, has its advantages for cruising.

Every so often when I'm bored with bars and websites and other typical ways to meet men, I take a little drive to a public rest stop about twenty miles away. It's a circular rest area, with separate sections for cars and large trucks, surrounded by tall trees and thick brush. There's a dilapidated, closed-down, cinder block bathroom in the center, the MEN and WOMEN signs now hidden by six vinyl porta-potties. Since it's set back from the interstate, dark and discreet and fairly empty between midnight and dawn, you can circle the old bathroom for hours looking for dick. Though cruising is heaviest in the warmer months, action is for the taking all year round.

Going to this place is not a habit for me, but occasionally I have a simple fetish that needs to be fed. A slight kink that has to be recognized or I'll explode; it's not common, and the only place for a five-foot-eleven, butch jock type to exhibit such a desire is a dark corner where no one is in a position to judge. Actually, it's a fetish so uncommon you can't find a website devoted to it.

Though I'm not into drag or cross-dressing, I happen to really get off on wearing black leather chokers, six-inch (or higher) black leather heels and black leather wristbands that can be hooked together like handcuffs. I love the combination of high heels and being bound and tied. There's something so hot about rough, black cowhide tugging the smooth skin on my neck; a thick choker so tight it runs along that thin line of discomfort; while my hands are clamped behind my back and a horny guy is giving me orders. My body is lean; I work out six days a week for a thirty-inch waist and a forty-three-inch chest. Legs long and shaved and tan, firm from endless hours of running nowhere on treadmills—the black leather high heels on me drive other guys wild. I work hard at submissiveness; I'm looking hot for strong, aggressive men who like to dominate.

One night last October when it was chilly and drizzly and damp, I decided to drive to the rest stop. Hadn't been there in months; not since the sultry night in June when I'd sucked off a couple of baggy-jeaned college guys who were too drunk to even remember it later, I'm sure. "Fuck, dudes, he drained my

cock...then licked me clean," said one. Sucking dirty dick, after
the typical ritual that was always so dangerous and exciting:
driving there wearing nothing but a belted black leather coat
that stopped just below my ass, six-inch black high heels and a
solid black leather, three-inch-wide choker. And, of course, black
leather wristbands. I always carried a bag with a T-shirt, jeans
and shoes for emergency, but half the fun was driving practically naked while wearing the high heels and choker, sometimes
turning on all the interior car lights and giving the older truck
drivers a cheap thrill.

Tie me up, boys; step on me; hold me down....

Normally I would have waited; lowered the passenger window to see if the other guy was interested or not, made eye contact with him. But I was feeling bold that night. I opened the
door, stepped out of the car and stood for a moment, adjusting
my belted coat to make sure you couldn't actually see my ass,
and pretending to check out the windshield wipers. Then I decided to show off a little, walking away from the car toward a
large metal trash can on the sidewalk, so the other guy could see
that I was practically nude. Not a feminine walk either; just a
normal guy with a good body who was completely at ease with
his fetish. It was extremely important to appear masculine and
bold, with a heavy step and legs always spread wide. I was ad-
vertising the body of a man...who just happened to be wearing
high heels and a choker.

Within minutes, as I walked toward a rain-soaked picnic
bench just beyond the trash can, I heard a car door slam shut
and I knew he liked what he'd seen. I turned and saw the guy
walking toward the picnic bench, too. He was tall and dark,
wearing a navy polo shirt and khaki slacks. He had the zipper
down and a fully erect cock poked from the opening. A hungry, delicious cock, I thought. He wouldn't even have to drop

his pants; just bend me over the picnic bench, lock my hands behind my back with the wristbands and fuck my brains out as fast as possible so that we could both get off and I could go home to bed.

As he approached, I leaned back against the picnic table spreading my legs, one dangling off the edge so he could look up my coat and see my dick and ass crack. Then I quickly decided to unfasten the belt on my coat. I opened it completely and let the fabric slide off my shoulders so that I was now sitting on the wooden table wearing nothing but black high heels and leather jewelry. With eager brown eyes, he pursed his lips as though he were about to whistle and took a deep breath.

When he reached the picnic table, he licked his index fingers and then slowly circled the tips of my nipples with his spit. "Suck me off," was all he said, as he spread his legs.

I extended my arms, nodding at the black wristbands. "Hook my hands behind my back first."

He smiled. From the front he took my hands, placed them behind my back and snapped the wristbands tightly so I couldn't move my arms at all. His hot breath was against my neck, his large and stiff cock rested against my thin waist.

I went down on my knees on the cracked concrete sidewalk. He unfastened his belt buckle, unbuttoned his khaki slacks, and yanked them down to his knees. His legs were real-man hairy; a dark fleece covering hard thigh muscles. I placed the palms of my hands on those thighs, opened my mouth, slowly stuck out my tongue and began to lick the tip of his dick.

"Ah yeah," he said, grabbing the leather choker and pulling me toward his crotch, "Suck me off real dirty and slow, bitch...."

I wrapped my wet lips around the head of his cock, sucking gently, tasting the salt and vinegar of his precum, swallowing as though the cream were juice. By that time I doubted the scene would be a full-force fuck session. He only wanted me to suck him off, which was fine with me.

"You're a dirty little cocksucker," he whispered, gently slapping the back of my head. "Such soft, smooth lips; you like being tied up and naughty." Then he slapped harder; his cock slammed my throat.

But then, just as I was about to begin the hard, wet sucking in order to get him off, he suddenly pulled away from my lips and looked to his left, toward the rest area entrance. Swiftly, he shoved his cock into his pants and then turned back toward the black sedan. Not speaking a word; not caring that I was bound with leather wristbands and couldn't move my arms. He walked quickly, got inside his car, started the engine and pulled away.

Though slightly offended at first (maybe he didn't like the high heels after all), I suddenly noticed headlights on the other side of the rest area. A police car: white with black letters and red lights. I knew the local police cruised the area in the summertime, hoping to bust men sucking dick, but I'd never seen one during the colder months. It wasn't busy enough for them to waste their time. I quickly put my coat between my teeth, knowing I wouldn't have enough time to get back to my car, and headed for one of the porta-potties, where I could unfasten the wristbands and hang out until the police car was gone. I knew the drill. They circled once, checking to see that no one was sucking dick in the wide open, and then left.

From a small crack in the plastic door of the porta-potty I saw the police car pull up next to my SUV and park. The driver then killed the engine, turned off the headlights and simply sat there. And for the next thirty minutes or so that's where he remained as I watched through the crack in the plastic door. I worked carefully to try and unhook the wristbands, but I couldn't seem to break free. My arms were hurting; I couldn't take the pain much longer. And then finally the snaps popped and I was free to move and put on my coat.

After sorting through my choices and realizing that I didn't want to sit in that awful porta-potty a minute longer, I finally decided to simply walk back to the car. I could have left the high heels inside, but I thought walking barefoot in November would seem even more suspicious. If he asked why I was walking around in nothing but a leather coat and high heels I'd say I had just come from a costume party; it was only one week till Halloween. I hadn't done anything wrong. There was a change of clothing in my car. As far as I knew, though embarrassing in the wrong context, high heels were not illegal.

As I opened the plastic door and stepped down, I put my hands in the pockets, trying to pull the coat longer, but it was futile. The coat barely covered my dick. All you could see were long, shaved, tanned legs and six-inch black high heels. Only several hundred feet to the car, but a walk of shame that felt like miles. And, oddly enough, I felt strangely excited, too.

Though I'd expected the cop to shine his headlights as I reached my car, he instead lowered his window and said, "Is everything all right?"

"Ah, yes, Officer," I said, my voice deep and butch and rough, "I was just coming from a Halloween party."

His expression was tongue in cheek; he knew there wasn't a Halloween party. Actually, I thought I noticed a half smile.

"Well, then you won't mind if I check your driver's license," he said, getting out of the patrol car.

"No, not at all. My wallet's on the front seat." Face-to-face, he was tall, six-feet-three or four, with short, dark, blond hair and a wide neck; delicate facial features that reminded me of a young Elvis Presley. A strong body built around massive shoulders covered by a uniform of light blue shirt and navy wool trousers. Large feet in heavy black leather cop shoes. If he hadn't been a football player in high school those muscles would have been a waste.

He opened my car door and said, "Why don't you reach in and get it."

I knew that if I bent over and reached for the wallet the coat would rise and expose my ass. "Can I just sit down in the car and hand it to you?"

"I said bend over and get the wallet," his voice was rough, but not mean.

He was asking for a show. So I turned, bent over and stretched my arms as far as they would reach, realizing that this encounter was becoming by far the hottest I'd ever had. Though he may have been ready to arrest me, I didn't care in the least. All I wanted was to show off my ass to the sexiest fucking cop I'd ever seen up close. The coat, as expected, rose to my waist and my bare, tanned ass was fully exposed. And then, as I grabbed the wallet, I felt the wool fabric of his slacks on my skin. His knee rubbing and pushing me down onto the black leather seat with gentle force. I spread my legs and arched my back inviting more. He gently lifted his leg and pressed the sole of his black shoe against my ass, tapping it a few times. I moaned and lifted my right leg, bending it at the knee so one high heel was in the air. He grabbed the heel of the shoe and rubbed it against his groin for a moment.

"Not wearing much under that coat I see," he said, now reaching down and running the palm of his large hand across my ass. Slowly, up and down and then back and forth, his thick middle finger circling the opening of my hole.

I dropped the wallet as he reached under my waist and slowly pulled me to a standing position, turning me so that I was facing him.

"This is a very warm coat," I said, looking directing into his sky blue eyes with an expression that said I'd do anything he wanted me to do.

He then began to unfasten the belt that held my coat together, opening it and allowing the leather to fall from my shoulders to the wet, cold parking lot. My cock was now fully erect. He grabbed me with his right hand, placed his left hand on my bare ass and then leaned forward to kiss me on the lips. I opened my mouth and his warm tongue began to circle mine. With force, he pulled me to his body and I wrapped both my arms around his wide shoulders. Then came some fast, hard face-sucking; his rough beard rubbing against my smooth chin. His thick dick, ready to burst from the navy wool slacks, was pressing against my exposed groin. He began to make fucking motions as though he were about to pound me into the metal frame of the car.

With my left hand holding his neck for support I reached down with my right hand and slowly began to unzip his pants. I felt the cold metal of his badge against my naked chest. I reached inside and grabbed his cock.

He bit my neck, just beneath the choker. "Oh, baby, that tastes like sweet candy. You're a cuddle toy."

"Handcuff me, I'll do whatever you want," I said, running my face across the cotton fabric of his pale blue uniform shirt, not knowing how he'd react. I began to rub his dick. A big cop cock. He smiled. "Turn around, boy."

As I turned, my arms already behind my back, he pulled out cold, shiny handcuffs and clamped my wrists together. I was now in complete submission; his fuck toy for as long as he wanted.

"Spread your legs," he ordered.

"Yes, Sir," I said.

"I'll just slip this big dick in and out real slow, baby," he said.

"I don't have any lube. You'll just have to bury that hard gun with your spit," I lied (there was a tube in the glove box).

"Shut the fuck up, bitch," he said, as he spit into the palm of his right hand and then rubbed the spit on his cock.

"Be gentle," I said, as he slammed the car door shut. The metal handcuffs clinked against the steel on his belt buckle.

I was now totally nude, save for the six-inch heels and choker, and he was fully clothed, with a thick cock swinging from the opening in his pants. Leaning over, I pressed my shoulders against the frame of the car, spreading my legs wide and arching my back. He spit again, lubed his cock and slowly began to work the head into my ass, which didn't resist much. His large hands held the sides of my smooth ass and he slowly began to fuck and pump and pound. The rough fabric of his uniform was rubbing against the back of my thighs, his outsized balls slapping the bottom of my ass.

"What's your name, boy?" he asked a few minutes later.

"Ricky," I replied, then asked, "What's your name, Officer?"

"Bobby," he replied, squeezing my ass so hard I knew there would be fingerprints and bruises the next day. I braced my legs firmly so I wouldn't lose my balance with the high heels on the wet pavement.

"Get ready, bitch," he shouted, fucking harder.

I knew he was ready to unload, and I was close, too. Actually, I'd been close to orgasm since the minute he'd shoved his cock up my hole and I'd had to hold back on purpose. I'd always been lucky; if the guy fucking me was rough enough, and he hit the right spots, I could climax without touching my dick. An internal orgasm: the best kind.

With his hand over my mouth, I began to moan, my tongue licking the palm of his large hand.

And then the fucking grew even more intense. With his free

hand he started to pull my ass toward his cock, practically lifting me in the air.

He grunted, skewering me on his dick; as he did I reached the best orgasm I'd ever had. The explosion wasn't just because of the high heels and choker, or being nude in a public rest area, or being fucked by a big strong cop. I craved the slight pain from the handcuffs; the rugged way he'd held my ass while he fucked. This was more than just a naughty-little-slut night for me. With this guy the action was *tie me up, kick me with your dirty boots and fuck my brains out so I can't walk tomorrow.*

For a moment, we remained in position. He gently ran the palms of his hands up and down my asscheeks, still slowly fucking me.

"You are the hottest thing I've ever seen, walking around out here in black leather high heels and choker collar."

I was slightly stunned. I'd expected him to jump off my back, pull up his zipper and say "Thanks." That's usually how the down low works. Then they go home to their girlfriends and wives.

He pulled out and unlocked the handcuffs. *Fuck dude*, I wanted to say, that was the best fucking pound session any guy ever gave me. I knew I'd still feel that big cock up my hole for days to come. He bent down, picked up my coat and helped pull my arms through the holes, pulling the belt tightly. Even after he'd fucked my brains out, he was still in control.

"I hope this doesn't sound weird," he said, running his hand up my ass again. "But my dick gets really hard when a good-looking guy wears high heels...stilettos really get me going. Do you think we can hook up again?"

I smiled. "Will you use the handcuffs?"

"Next time I'll completely dominate you—you on your back, hands tied to the bedpost, a gag in your mouth and those high heels over my shoulders...."

I found paper and a pen in the car, wrote my number and handed it to him. He reached down and ran both hands under my coat, resting them on my ass. "I'll call you tomorrow," he said, his blue eyes sparkling with satisfaction.

THE ART OF
THE SUTURE

Brooke Stern

I write this memoir with humility, for I have only the smallest footnote to contribute to the literature of bondage. I write to describe a most unusual practice—a lost art, even—that I perfected out of necessity during the last world war. Having long since disappeared, this practice may be lost to history if I fail to describe it and the historical circumstances that led to its invention. Though it's an artifact of a bygone era and unwise to resurrect, I write of a practice not without some charms, a practice that brought great pleasure, as well as some pain, to its practitioners. It is, in my judgment, worth recording, and thus I begin my tale.

I had just finished my long apprenticeship and opened my own tailor shop when the war began. That meant I had very few clients. The older men had already established relationships with their tailors and were reluctant to switch, while the young men were all away in the army. Not to mention the economic hardships that had struck and the disruptions in trade that affected our supplies of cloth. People were forsaking new clothes. Wearing the same suits and dresses several years in a row became something of a statement of character. Decadence had gone out of style, or rather the concept had gone underground and existed in only the most rarified circles. Needless to say, no members of those circles frequented my shop.

I was only days away from accepting my failure and returning, humbled, to the tailor for whom I'd apprenticed when a young man came by my shop with an odd request. He had heard, correctly, that the craftsmanship of my hems and seams was among the best. He asked me if I had ever done seams for ladies' clothing. I couldn't see his purpose in this question, for a good seam, meant to be unseen and discreet, was no different for women than for men. I reassured him that I had, though I hadn't actually done any women's garments. I was desperate, and there was nothing he could ask me to do that was beyond me. Next, he asked me if I was familiar with the situation concerning ladies' stockings at that moment, and I replied truthfully that I was. It was well known that all natural and synthetic elastic, as well as all silk, was being monopolized by the military. Without elastic or silk, it was therefore almost impossible to get stockings that conformed to the shape of a lady's legs. Indeed, some of the atrocities that passed for stockings in those days were as baggy as men's trousers. Finally, he asked me if I was familiar with the most recent trend among society women to address the lack of stockings. I thought it likely that he would call my bluff if I lied, so I replied that I was not, hoping it wouldn't preclude me from his business. Ladies of means who were determined to look attractive for whatever reason (he said this with both a sneer and a smile) were having stockings that would otherwise be quite baggy sewn together while on their legs so as to achieve the form-fitting tightness so desired. The seam, following the shape of the leg and determining the ultimate success or failure of the effect, had to be of the finest quality, and the patience and skill of the tailor were of paramount importance.

I could see why. I thought I had never heard of a more appetizing assignment. I assured him I was eager to try my hand at the task and could guarantee him that my seam would have no equal. This pleased him, and we agreed that he would bring a lady by the following week to have her stockings sewn up prior to a ball that evening. I would procure the best material I could for these stockings (for which he advanced me a generous sum) and would block off several hours for the long process of sewing a seam up the contours of this woman's legs.

You can imagine my eagerness as well as my hopes of this lady's attractiveness. Indeed, I was optimistic for I assured myself that no man would pay such a sum for this service if the lady in question were unattractive. When the day arrived, I awaited her anxiously, having exceeded my budget to make sure I had the finest black market silk. It was amazingly fine and beautifully translucent. I knew that the ball to which the gentleman referred wasn't going to be a normal affair. The style at traditional balls still involved dresses so large and elaborate that the shape of a leg hardly mattered. No, this was another sort of thing completely—the sort of thing members of my social class only could read about in prurient novels.

When the door of my store finally opened, a woman entered who possessed beauty, grace, youth and daring in proportions that I had never imagined possible. She arrived alone, saying the gentleman had no patience for the long procedure that was about to occur. She told me exactly what he wanted her to be wearing, the exact effect on her curves it was to have, and asked if I minded if she smoked while I worked. I told her I didn't mind at all and went to fetch my newest, sharpest needles. When I returned, she had let the skirt she was wearing fall to her feet and stood, statuesque, in nothing but a blouse, knickers, and suspenders awaiting something to suspend. It is hard for another to imagine the thrill I received when I thought about spending the next hours in direct contact with those legs, my head close enough to that crotch that I would smell it like I smelled the blossoming garden outside my window.

Indeed, that is exactly how I spent the next hours, careful to do the finest quality work and not to do anything that might dissuade her from utilizing my services again. I instructed her that if she removed the stockings carefully by severing the thread I was now sewing, she could return the silk to me for reuse. Though I had pulled it so taut that it would inevitably be stretched, I thought I could still sew it onto a woman slightly larger than the one I had just sewn into it. When she put her dress back on and left that day, I watched her legs as she walked out of my store and thought proudly that no one could possibly know from looking at those legs that we lived in an era when silk and elastic were scarce.

When the next week began, I awaited the return of the gentleman, who had promised he would come to pay the bill. I desperately hoped he would schedule another appointment. I was quite beside myself, not daring to imagine a future of women's legs in my shop but hoping for it nonetheless. He finally returned, on Wednesday and well after I had given up and figured that I would never see the money I was owed. He announced that he was terribly pleased with my efforts and asked if I could possible manage to do the same thing for three women this coming Friday. Three! This truly exceeded my expectations. I told him I could, but only on the condition that the first arrive at seven in the morning. He replied that she would. I was hesitant to ask about the silk from last week's stockings but did so anyway, as I would have to know whether it was going to be returned to me if I were to assess my need for new supplies. He admitted to me that the silk had become quite unusable due to certain activities, but offered to compensate me generously. This he did, tipping me as well.

That Friday was an embarrassment of riches. I didn't know my gentleman benefactor's name, nor did I know the names of the women whose every contour from thigh to toe I became intimately familiar with. But they were all quite pleased with my handiwork and left glowing with the feeling of being glamorous and finely dressed for perhaps the first time in a year. That they were not women of the finest classes and probably dependent on their gentleman friends to finance their glamor should go without saying. They were actresses, starlets or faux ingénues whose beauty, charm and freedom elevated them to the objects of desire of the highest class of men. These men led double lives that were secrets to no one: propriety, titles and progeny on the one hand; these women, their soirees and nights no one asked about on the other. That it was an arrangement to everyone's satisfaction was quite obvious to me.

Soon, this became my main trade and I was approached by many gentlemen about providing my services to the ladies in their keep. I noted that no silk was ever returned to me and surmised that a great part of the allure of this odd sartorial bondage was the thrill that must have been attained by violently ripping the lady free of it. I imagined my creations—some three to four hours in the making—being destroyed in a few seconds of passion. I was foreplay for them, I thought; my sewing, an essential part of the long ritual preceding the final release. I thought this not only because of my insights into human sexuality, but also because of the smell of the ladies' arousal that emanated from between their legs as they passed the tedium of their day by imagining how their night would end. Sometimes I was sorely tempted to offer them a degree of satisfaction to help pass the time, but I was too afraid to do anything that might disrupt my wonderfully rejuvenated cash flow.

There was still, however, the small matter of the war and so it was not all smooth going. Some of the young men who were patrons of these women were called up for duty and faced the imminent prospect of leaving their women behind. Knowing the ease with which these women could be stolen from them in their absence (for many of these men had acquired their women by theft in the first place), some of the men were determined to go to whatever length necessary to assure that their treasures would faithfully await their return. The men were aware that the greatest threat they faced for their lovers' fidelity came from the soirees themselves. The women, knowing when and where they were held, could easily return and find new lovers, lovers present to lavish them with gifts and pleasures, not far away and in peril. The men's options were equally bad: either unenforceable interdictions against their lovers attending the soirees or blind trust that their lovers might—drunk, poor and alone—resist temptation.

One of these gentlemen approached me with a suggestion. After announcing that he was going to ship out to North Africa, he told me that he fully expected that when he left, Laura, his lover, would come to me the following week spending some other man's money to get her legs done up. He therefore wanted to continue to reserve my services to prepare her stockings for every party on the social calendar so that she'd have no basis for complaints of neglect or deprivation. This was not, however, all he wanted me to do. He asked me if I could do anything to guarantee him that his Laura wouldn't stray.

When I asked him what he had in mind, he paused and professed not to have really given it much thought. When I pressed him, however, he proposed a plan in great detail, one so cunning and well thought out that I had to do little more than get over my moral qualms and implement it. He wished me to sew longer stockings on Laura, the sort that would now be called hosiery. They wouldn't need suspenders because they would go all the way up. These would be tapered at the waist and therefore impossible to pull down without tearing the top part of the seam. She would thereby be trapped in her stockings until she came to me to remove them and to certify her chastity.

As if this weren't enough, this gentleman was a bit of a sadist, so he had an additional measure in mind. He was afraid that she could still remove the stockings and simply have them resewn by another tailor. I wanted to assure him that my seams had no equal and that I could certainly detect an imposter, but I kept silent in order to hear the rest of his plan. In order to prevent such an actuality, he insisted that I make small stitches in the flesh of her buttocks, so as to remind her of her obligation to him and dissuade her from any impulse to remove the stockings during the evening. I could therefore be certain that there had been no removal and replacement of her stockings by inspecting the state of the wound. Moreover, he wondered if I could put a small patch of loose mesh underneath her crotch so that urine could flow freely through, all the while guaranteeing that she would return to me late the very night of the soiree and not go home with another gentleman for she would need her stockings removed sooner rather than later if she were to need to attend to what he delicately referred to as her other needs. This would require me to stay quite late in my shop, something he would, of course, compensate me for.

Furthermore, the plan would depend entirely on my discretion. I would be in a highly corruptible position, he pointed out, what with desperate, guilty women willing to do anything so that I wouldn't report their transgressions to their lovers far from home. He warned that he might test my honesty by sending a woman to me who professed to be in such a situation. I assured him that I would be unimpeachable and asked if he would like to witness the trial run of his plan that coming Friday.

He accepted my invitation and that Friday he and Laura arrived in the afternoon, my last appointment of the day. Previously, I had turned a butler's blind eye to the nature of the relationship between the gentlemen and the ladies they brought to me. Furthermore, I had always been certain to act with a tailor's trained indifference to the body upon which he is fitting his clothes. I had pretended not to notice the sometimes conspicuous age difference between the men and their feminine company. I had never inquired as to the background of the women with whom I spent my day, nor had I made any effort at conversation at all. I had acted as if each were the highest born lady, responding to them when they were alone and let their accents slip the same way I did when they spoke like the queen in the presence of their gentlemen escorts. In short, I had never done anything to make the women anxious or inhibited as I spent many hours so near to their exposed bodies that I knew every freckle, every smell, every hair on it. I had never done anything that I thought might imperil my privileged position in the employ of their gentlemen, for I knew that a whisper from the lady about me would cause them all to go running to another tailor.

But that refined indifference to the bodies and the positions of the women upon whom I sewed stockings was bound to change with the appointment that Friday. I was to be their gentlemen's proxy. I was to be the custodian of their feminine flesh in the gentlemen's absence. I was the enforcer of their virtue. My stitches, a fashion accessory the previous week, were to become an instrument of the gentlemen's sadism and a marker of his property. The captivity of the women, once an unspoken arrangement, was to become pierced into the flesh of their soft, alabaster buttocks. They were property, privileged chattel; and I, the groundskeeper of the gentlemen's domain.

Moreover, the bodies that I had previously been so careful to ignore were to become my focus. My cultivated sense of indifference, no matter how dishonest, to the fine, private parts of the body would be shattered, as I would need to direct all my attention, plus an extra degree of personal sadism, to fulfill my duty. I would be far from indifferent as I pinched the fleshiest crown of each buttock and pierced it with my finest needle, pushing inward toward the crack and under the surface of the skin until I brought the needle out a fraction of an inch away, creating a stitch unlike any other I had ever seen.

I had been imagining it all week. I had speculated on the consistency of flesh under my needle. I had even wondered if I should practice first on myself, but in the end my disinclination to feel pain won out over my desire to feel well-prepared. Laura's flesh was the first I ever pierced with a needle. It was lovely flesh that belonged to an equally lovely woman.

Laura had always been friendlier with me than most women. She had joked and smoked and chatted the hours away when I would be sewing her stockings. She understood her position and did nothing to pretend to be something that she wasn't. So, on that Friday, when she mounted the platform upon which she always stood when I sewed her stockings, it didn't surprise me that she lowered her knickers without hesitation, pulling them down below her knees and then lifting her feet one at a time before handing me the small, luxurious bit of silk and lace to put aside. She wouldn't need them again until she returned to me after the night out. I admired them and put them aside, smelling distinctly the traces of excitement emanating from them, an excitement that could only have been a fraction of my own.

It seemed to take forever for my seam to climb the length of her legs. Finally, I was higher than I had ever been before, up above where her suspenders would have been and up to where I couldn't help but touch her where I had never touched her before. Each time my fingers grazed the hair between her legs, I had to discreetly dry them on my own trousers. I could only conclude that my patron's sadism was matched by his mistress's affection for her ordeal. I fitted the stockings around her waist, stitched up the seams that linked the various pieces of silk be-tween her legs and proceeded up the seam that went up the crack of her bottom. The piece of loose mesh that I placed in her crotch would serve its purpose well, letting urine through without offering even the least endowed man the opportunity of entry without tearing it. Finally, I was done. The moment had arrived. I paused and she looked down at me, took a long drag on her cigarette, exhaled, and waited.

"Well, go on then," she said.

I lowered my eyes to the flesh of her buttocks and swabbed it with alcohol the way I had seen doctors do. Then I took her flesh between the fingers of my left hand and guided the needle in with my right, as smoothly and gently as I could. I felt her gasp and struggle not to tense her buttock.

"Almost done," I said. It was a lie that I would repeat end-lessly throughout my career. A dot of blood trickled from the spots where the needle entered and exited. I had a scrap of clean cotton on hand to dab it. When the blood continued, I pressed the cotton on the flesh and held it there on her but-tock for several minutes, all the while reflecting on the dizzying reality of attending to the most intimate parts of this woman's body and the most private parts of her life. After repeating the procedure on her other buttock and helping her dress without unnecessarily disturbing the healing wounds, we awaited her lover's return. After a long silence, she said something I would never forget.

"Once he's gone, you'll be the only man who can give me what I need."

I was so young and inexperienced then that I didn't know what to say. Was this something that her lover had told her to say so as to test my behavior? What was it she needed? What would she ask of me? Her lover arrived before I could get answers to any of these questions, but over the next months, I came to learn the answers many times over. Indeed, I have Laura to thank for my understanding of the intricacies of a woman's anatomy.

She must have found me equally satisfying, because word spread about these additional services as well. Indeed, there were many women who had unmet needs now that their men were at war. The most unusual thing, though, was the nature of these needs. If they had simply needed sex or money or attention, they could have gotten them anywhere, but what it seemed they needed was something a good bit more specific. They needed the ritual of their untying—even more intense now that it involved unbinding their flesh itself—to get them off, to prime them, and once primed, they needed to fuck to come down off their frantic high. They had come to pair the untying and the sex so tightly that one without the other became quite unimaginable. No man without my skill at stitching and unstitching could satisfy them.

Far more frequent than the occasional woman who came anxious to pay me off to cover for a tryst with another man (I never accepted such bribes) were the women who had behaved well throughout the night, only to beg me to fuck them after I had delicately undone their seams. By the time they had stood on my tailor's pedestal dreaming of what used to be done to them after those stockings came off, they were quite beside themselves with desire. It was after the evening of restraining their every urge that they arrived on my doorstep, knowing that I was their only hope, the one person so deep in the trust of their gentlemen, so unsupervised, and so corruptible. If they were going to get their needs attended to, it would be by me. And more often than not, I acquiesced.

At first, I was nervous that one of the men would try to entrap me but that turned out to be an empty threat. Maybe they hadn't gotten around to planning ahead or maybe they couldn't find a woman willing to get her ass flesh sewn just to inspect the workings of my shop. Indeed, apart from my own indulgence, I adhered more-or-less strictly to the gentlemen's requests, enforcing the women's fidelity and inspecting their stockings for any sign of mischief. The ones who claimed a toileting emergency were subject to the sort of examination that might detect sexual activity. The first exams I gave, like the first sutures, then, occurred in my role as tailor, not medical student. The ones who didn't show up at all or who showed evidence of sexual activity got reported to their lovers at war, even after all the tears and pleas to forgive her just this once.

On the rare occasion, if I liked a girl, I would let her off with a harsh spanking and a warning never to let it happen again, but generally I knew that this sort of leniency would come back to bite me if offered too freely. So as much as I enjoyed administering the spankings on the already wounded bottoms, I generally restrained myself and did as I had been instructed.

Sometimes a woman would disappear entirely. I would later hear that she had gone off with another man and had no intention to even try and deceive. In fact, some men took great pride making women break their vows: "to unthread," "to come undone," or "to undo" came to mean that you had convinced a woman to take out her stitch and fuck you, at the expense of obvious discovery. The four small spots of blood that stained the sheets when she had been fucked on her back were treasured as mementos of the accomplishment. "To tie the knot" and other expressions took on a whole new meaning as well.

When the war finally ended, these practices were among the many things that suddenly became outdated, obsolete, and, truthfully, better off forgotten. I had become quite good at sewing a suture, though, and easily got a job at a veteran's hospital. There, I learned enough of the basics of anatomy, pathology and medicine to apply to medical school and be accepted. But I never forgot my time as a tailor, and I never once sutured up a flesh wound without recalling my delectable training.

UNLOCKING

Zaedryn Meade

W hat's this key for?" Maya asks, fingering the smallest key on the key chain clipped to my belt loop. I toss back the last mouthful of whiskey she brought me earlier, now watered down from the melted ice.

"It's a handcuff key," I say, watching her face for a reaction. I don't usually reveal my interest in bondage to a girl I haven't even kissed yet, not knowing if it might scare her away. But her eagerness to reciprocate for the drink I bought her and the way she responded to my rough lead on the dance floor hint that she's interested.

"Really," she says. Her wide brown eyes flash gold and reveal her desire. "I've never been handcuffed before."

I don't miss that invitation. "Would you like to be?"

Her hips switch and tilt. Oh yeah, she wants to be. Possibly even by me. "I don't know," she says slowly, placing herself closer to me with every imperceptible movement. Her fingers are still in my belt loop and she's pulling at the circle around my hips. I'm leaning back into it and making her lean into me. She tilts her face up toward mine, a good four inches shorter than my not-so-tall five foot six, and does that doe-eyed, under-the-eyelashes look of girls who want to be kissed.

I reach behind her to set my glass on the tall table, changing places with her. She turns too and now her back is to the wall. She leans against it and hooks both thumbs into her pockets, holding her bottle of Corona by the neck in her left hand. Only the lime at the bottom is left.

I take the bottle out of her hand and use that as an opportunity to touch her skin. I set the bottle on the table next to my empty glass, barely looking to see where it lands, eyes locked on Maya's dark thick eyelashes and smoky makeup. She's biting her lip. I have the back of her hand in mine and press her palm with my thumb. Her fingers are a little colder than her wrist.

My thumb and forefinger circle her wrist and I squeeze, just a little, enough pressure to let her feel restricted. I take her other hand, notice that she's already reaching for me, and do the same. She breathes in, a little surprised at the sudden movement. I press her wrists back until they touch the wall and see the tension in her shoulders. Her breasts are offered up to me like fruit to suck on in order to bring out the flavor of the whiskey, and she knows it, sees me considering her and arches further. I want to press my palm into the ripeness of her chest and feel the flesh pushed between my palm and the wall. I want to take a bite of the taut muscles of her neck. I want to run my tongue from her chin down past the collar of her thin cotton blouse and into the V of her neckline where she has one too many buttons undone.

I don't do any of these things. I keep my eyes on her face as she tells me what she wants, what she's afraid to give away, what she wishes I'd keep doing to her, without saying a word.

Maya's mouth makes a sweet, high whimper that is quickly

cut off by my own mouth pressing into hers. She pushes her hips into mine and makes a move in to kiss me that is more sudden than I expected, and I almost lose my balance and my grip around her wrists. I pull her hands behind her back and they touch easily; her wrists are thin enough to get locked in one of my hands, so I bring my left hand to the back of her neck, along her spine and under her long dark hair. Her body arches and she kisses me harder, her tongue beginning to feather my lips. I open my mouth, catch her swollen bottom lip between my teeth gently, then pull away and touch her lips as lightly as possible. She's pressing toward me for more but I'm holding her back by her wrists.

She struggles against my grip and almost gets one wrist free before I catch it in my left hand. She smiles against my mouth, flexes her fingers and stops struggling. I pull back and she's still smiling. I let go and she brings her hands between us, touches one wrist with the other, then pulls on my keys again.

"Take me home with you," she says.

I grin.

Circling her right wrist with my left hand, I lead her back through the pulsing bodies on the dance floor, and out the front door of the bar.

I get nervous when we arrive at my small studio apartment, like I always do. I start overthinking things and worrying that I'm not being enough of a host, that I don't even know this girl, that I've misread her. She gazes at the framed black-and-white nude portrait photographs on the walls, her hands cupped behind her back like she's wandering through a museum. Or as though she is offering her wrists to me to bind.

After rustling through the small wooden chest next to my bed, I come up behind her, my face in her hair. She smells amazing, some musky-floral scent from her crème rinse or perfume, and I push her hands in front of her with my thumbs and first fingers in an *L* shape. She catches sight of the cuffs dangling from my fingertips and touches them lightly, turning the leather over in her hand, feeling the metal clasp and chain that link the two loops of leather together.

"My best friend's a photographer," I say, my arms around her as I open one cuff in each of my hands as an invitation. "She always gives me photos as gifts. These are my favorites." My lips are touching her ear as I speak, then the line of her jaw, then her neck.

She sighs and slips her wrists into the cuffs one at a time as I keep them stable. "I like this one," she says, indicating an abstract close-up of a neck and shoulder blade, her back arching again, turning her head a little. She wants to kiss me. I can see her lips part, her breath getting shallow and quicker.

I snap the cuffs closed with the thin sound of metal on metal. "They'll stay closed without being locked," I say, "but if you pull them apart, hard, they'll open."

She considers this. I want her to have the option of a quick out, in case she panics. The cuffs will still hold in place through quite a bit of pressure and pulling, and she tests this by pulling her wrists apart slightly. They don't open.

"Will you lock them?" she says in a small voice, turning to face me but keeping her eyes low. She has such submissive instincts. This is going to be beautiful.

I unclip my keys from my belt loop and take the small silver key between my fingers. I hold her hands up between us and watch her face as I lock each wrist closed, then clip the keys back onto my jeans. She raises her arms up and I circle her tiny waist with my arms while she settles her hands behind my head, forearms on my shoulders. Our mouths meet again and it is sweet, tender, hungry. She presses against me hard and my keys dig into my hip bone. She's on her toes to reach me and wants to bring her legs around my waist. I can tell by the way her hips are opening and how she easily, eagerly lets me lift her thigh with the slightest touch of my hand as her knee bends and the small heel of her sandal finds the back of my knee.

Taking a few steps backward, I pull Maya along with me until we are next to the tan couch against the wall. I sit back and she bends from the waist, then moves one leg at a time to either side of my hips, kneeling over me, placing her still restrained hands behind my head. Our faces are close and her hair is falling in her eyes; I push it behind her ears with my fingers, then trace the line of her blouse down to its first button, three of them already unbuttoned, slipping it through its buttonhole. She kisses me. I am beginning to identify the taste of her mouth, behind the lime and Corona. She tastes like the night air in summer when it's about to turn fall and the trees are beginning to shiver their leaves. I still taste like whiskey.

Her hips are working up and down on mine like we are already fucking, like I am already inside her, like I have a cock inside my jeans and she is ready to milk it till I come.

I get her blouse undone but of course it won't come off over the cuffs, so I just slip it off her shoulders and it catches at her elbows, which further restricts her movement and frames her collarbone, cleavage, and cute light-pink bra nicely. Her breasts are small, the bra more for shape than support (unlike my own), but are comfortable handfuls and lovely, round and full. Her nipples are hard already. Maya's skin starts to sheen with sweat. My lust is building strong, my clothes are getting tight. I want to take my lips to her nipples. I want to see her breasts bound with rope.

Maneuvering her onto her back on the couch, I twist and set

the weight of my body between her legs as she presses her hips up to meet me. My keys are still sharp against my hip. I bring a hand up to hold the cuffs above her head and she inhales, her stomach tightening.

"Oh god, you feel so good," she whispers through the thickness of her desire, when I lower my mouth to her breastbone and push her bra off of her darkening nipple. It contracts in my mouth and I work it like a clit, flicking it with my tongue, lapping in broad strokes. She presses her hips into me and moans.

"Can I take your jeans off?" I say quietly, letting go of her wrists to tug at the waist of her jeans. She nods.

I pull them off easily, revealing tiny cream-colored panties, satin and thin, which I leave on. I pull my own black T-shirt over my head to reveal a very plain black bra. She sits up, intending to take it off of me, but can't reach her bound hands around me to get to the clasp. She realizes this quickly.

I indicate her wrists. "Do you like those?"

She nods, a little embarrassed by her own submission. "Yes," she says. She pulls at my keys, touches my stomach. I step up off the couch and go back to the toy box.

"I have some rope," I say. "Can I bind you?" I can feel the questions in her face with my back turned. What would I bind? Her wrists, her ankles? Would she like it? Would I fuck her while she was bound, or after?

From the toy box I remove two twelve-foot lengths of black rope wrapped in neat bundles. Maya is sitting up on the couch, white blouse pulled down around her elbows, wrists in her lap. I set one of the ropes on the bed and bring the other over to her. In a flourish of movement designed to look impressive, I shake the rope free from its bundle. She watches me as I kneel on the wood floor in front of her, between her legs.

We are nearly eye to eye this way. I set the rope on the couch and unclick my key ring. I touch her hands, lightly running my fingers over her soft skin, and she shivers. Her hands have become an erogenous zone. She shuts her eyes.

I lick my lips. "Are you ready?"

She nods. I sit back on my heels and unlock the cuffs one at a time, then set the keys aside and take each of her hands in mine, kissing her wrists, the bones in her fingers, her swirled fingerprints. I raise to my knees and she reaches for me, melting against me, trusting my grip on her and giving me a serious hard-on by wrapping her legs around my waist again, pulling me back. I get hold of the thin, soft fabric of her white blouse and manage to remove it, along with her bra. She pulls at the rope next to her, tangles her hand in it.

"What are you going to do to me?" she asks, barely breathing, eyes wide and begging for it, whatever it is. She doesn't even know, but she hopes it involves her getting tied up and fucked. She didn't even know she wanted that until tonight, until right now.

I stand and pull her to her feet. I drape the length of rope over her shoulder and drag it along her bare skin. The sensation, the movement, is tiny, but so specific that every nerve in her skin feels it.

"First, I'm going to bind your breasts in a chest harness, which will look like an X across your chest." I kiss the top of her shoulder, then my mouth moves to the arc where her breast meets her chest. I roll one nipple in between my fingers as I continue to slowly pull on the rope, moving it over her stomach. "Then, if you want it, I'm going to bind you here," I say, gently pulling the rope between her thighs, letting it graze the fabric of her panties and her swelling cunt. "If you want it," I say again.

"I want it," she whispers, nearly whimpering. "Yes, I want it," she adds, to be sure I am clear. Her eyes are closed and she's keeping her breathing low and even. The urge to lunge for me is clear. She doesn't want it to end and she wants more, wants to feel it all over, wants to feel her muscles pull against restraints.

I smile. "Good. Hold this here," I say, finding the thin red ribbon tied to indicate the midpoint of the rope and placing it right between her breasts. "Just for a minute while I start the binding." I fight the urge to toss the rope on the floor and kiss her, hold her, fuck her, feel the muscles of her cunt and watch her face as I make her come.

Maya keeps the midpoint between her breasts, and I drape the ends over her shoulders, wrapping them under her arms and under her breasts, crossing the ends under the loop of the midpoint. She watches me in the heavy mirror hanging on one wall, near the room's only closet, as I weave the rope around her small breasts, crisscrossing until it curls around her like ivy, finding every possible place to cling. Then I'm done. She's bound; I stand back to admire my work.

"How does that feel?" I ask, running two fingers between the rope and her skin, testing the tension.

She breathes out and closes her eyes. "Good."

"Not too tight?" I say.

She considers. "No."

"Breathe in deep. Make your lungs full," I say. She does. The rope barely constricts her, only just at the end of the inhale. I smile. "Lovely."

"It's...good," she says again, already near panting, turned on, sipping hard at the air around her as her chest expands and contracts. Her eyes are sheened with diamonds, sparkling, her face upturned and opening, wanting. Her body's sensitivity is already heightened; she's waiting for me to touch her.

I continue to run two fingers between the ropes and her skin, one hand on her lower back so she can use me for support. Her skin is creamy, caramel and ivory, fine and thin as white-sand beaches and I feel as though I could dip my fingers inside, pull out tiny shining treasures. She ripples under my touch.

"You look beautiful," I say, lowering my mouth to suck on her shoulder, her neck, her collarbone. She leans into me and moans. I stand behind her, wrapping my arms around her, cupping her breasts in my palms, touching my lips to her skin everywhere I can reach.

"You feel amazing," she says, her breath part air and part moan. "So amazing. My skin is so alive."

"One more length of rope, and you can relax," I offer, moving to the bed to retrieve my second twelve-foot length of rope. Maya follows, keeping the distance between us close.

I position myself behind her again, gently peeling her cream-colored panties off of the perfect roundness of her asscheeks, making my hips twitch and my internal cock harden; my desire is hard to manage. I want to feel her long, slender fingers on the shaft of my strap-on, want to watch her ride my hips, want to feel myself thrusting inside her. I want her mouth on my fingers, on my clit. I try to fight the raw urges and begin to bind her again, quicker this time. I run my fingers over her smooth belly, over her hips and thighs, careful to avoid her cunt; I want to wait until we can't wait any longer.

I find the midpoint of the second rope and grip it in my palm, folded. I press her legs apart with my knees and she strengthens her legs and spreads wide. I press my hand between her legs, still avoiding touching her cunt, and thread the rope through to my left hand in front of her.

"Will you hold this, here, please?" I ask, pressing a tiny bit on the midpoint, now placed at the top of her pubic hair, to indicate where to hold the rope. Her hair is trimmed and neatly edged, thick though, and dark, like the hair on her head. I try not to imagine what she'll taste like, how she'll move and moan, how she'll let me take her, how far in she'll let me go.

She holds the rope in place and I gently trace the rope with my fingers as it disappears between her legs, between her labia; finding her hole wet, dripping, slicking the rope immediately, swollen with want. I kneel and trace my fingers alongside the rope, gently tickling her labia this time with my fingertips, pulling the folds of her out of the way and placing the slim rope just where I want it: parting her slick lips and opening her for the taking.

She is quiet, controlling her desire with even breaths. I wrap each of the two ends of the rope around each hip, then under the midpoint she's holding, waiting. The ends pull the small amount of slack in the rope taut and pull open her labia further, making a triangle out of the rope, mirroring the triangle of hair between her legs. Each end of rope then runs over her hips and behind her back, crossed at the small of her back, and tied in front, a few inches below the rope binding her breasts, just above her belly button.

I test the rope's tightness again, pulling on the line across her hips, then at her cunt, slipping my fingers between her legs. She's so soft and tender, so trusting, and she doesn't really even know me. It's beautiful and touching that I could be so trustworthy, that I could be handed the power to control, to invade, to be inside of this gorgeous creature, open before me. I want to feel every inch of her skin. I can't wait; the knots are tied, the rope is on, she's mine; I have to take her. I circle the opening of her hole with my fingers, slip one inside her with no effort, and add another. She shudders against me, gasping.

"Yes—" she whispers, barely audible. "Oh yes, do that, more, again."

My mouth waters. She grips my hand, the one that's inside

her. I kiss her, hard, slide another finger inside and slowly move them in and out, curling my knuckles to massage the walls of her cunt. Her mouth is greedy and she sucks my tongue, bites my lip, opens wide to let me taste her. She presses her body to mine and the ropes are hard, a little surprising, biting into the skin of my stomach.

"Oh god, fuck me, yes do that—there—" she's close to coming already, her cunt contracting around my fingers and pulling them deeper inside of her. I manage to get her to the bed and lay her down. She brings one arm overhead immediately and grips the headboard, keeping one hand on mine that is still inside her, touching her clit with her fingers. She moans, closes her eyes, her face open mouth open cunt open palms of her hands open and she's gasping, breathing hard. She takes my fingers in deeper and I can feel everything, every rippling muscle. Her stomach contracts and pulls at her breasts, shimmering, her nipples are hard and darkened. I catch one with my mouth. Flick it with my tongue and suck. Her fingers are working her clit and I'd like to watch but it's not about me, it's about her body now, about how she's telling me to open her creases, her corners, her locked boxes.

Maya comes, grasping, growling, pushing her cunt into my hand, hard; as her thighs jerk back, knees bent and angled, pulling her body into a fetal crunch, stomach contracting, muscles pulling and releasing over and over until she's moaning, nearly whimpering, chest heaving against the ropes, hips wide and pressed to the bed, eyes still closed. She quiets and I leave my mouth on her skin, my tongue on the spaces where the ropes crisscross the tightest; press my body thick and warm next to hers and she curls around me, presses into my jeans, my chest; drapes her fingertips over the skin of my back and neck, across the shortest hair on the back of my head. My fingers find the rope knotted under her breasts, on her stomach, and I work it loose, pulling slack into the tight bindings. She sighs, nuzzles a little into me, smiles into my neck.

Later, after she is untangled and has pulled her tiny cream-colored satin panties back on, her jeans, her light-pink bra, her white blouse, the sandals on her delicate feet, she looks at me again with those doe-eyes, that look not just like she wants me to kiss her but as if she wants me to keep kissing her, tomorrow, next week, in her bed, in the park, when she steps out of a car. But I don't really know anything about this girl, and she doesn't know me. She wants to ask to see me again, but swallows the words and the flavor of my whiskey in the back of her throat instead.

Maya leaves a scrap of paper on the top of my dresser that reads: *Next time I'm in charge—Maya*. Her phone number beneath her name.

On her tiptoes in the doorway she kisses me, tilts her face up toward mine, those impossibly wide brown eyes soft and golden, shining, clear. She looks shy for a moment, then whispers, "This is going to sound terrible, but...what's your name again?"

"Zed," I say. "My name's Zed."

ABRAHAM

James Walton Langolf

She is his Isaac laid out on the hood of his Ford—open, bared to his blade.

She gave him the knife in the bar parking lot, the textured grip already worn smooth from some other guy's back pocket.

He was sitting on a corner stool watching her out on the dance floor going through partners like she got them on special.

She was playing it hard, grinding her crotch up against theirs, rubbing them all over with her tits, but it was him she was watching when she pushed those dark sweaty curls out of her eyes. He could see these guys panting, smell their testosterone and disappointment over the smoke and spilled beer, like blood left on slow boil.

She watched him for an hour, maybe more as he was drinking shot after shot of cheap whiskey and she was murdering whole battalions with her wriggling ass. Hell, he saw one guy staggering away with a wet spot spreading across his fly.

Then, of course, "Buy me a drink?"

"Sure," he said, and she cocked an eyebrow at the barmaid who already had the tequila pouring. She was ready with the salt and the lime.

She squeezed the lime onto the back of her hand then dusted it with salt, but instead of sucking, she pulled her skin between her teeth and bit down hard. She was looking him in the eye and he didn't breathe while she was gnawing her own hand to the bone.

"Jesus Christ, lady."

She knocked back the shot and did the brow thing for another.

They were making small talk while he was hypnotized by the indentations of her teeth in her hand. He could hear knuckles cracking all around the room, hear pool cues thumping against the floor. Her hand was on his thigh and he was thinking, "Well, we're really gonna get into it now." Whatever "it" was.

She wore a ring on her left hand that she didn't even try to hide.

She snuck a hand under the table and into his pocket, her fingertips brushing his throbbing cock. He choked on a groan and she pulled out his keys, jangling them on their furry green rabbit's foot chain.

"Give them back."

She laughed and jangled them again, the sound grating against his nerves that were already too close to the skin.

"Give them back."

She mimed dropping them down her blouse and he grabbed her wrist, squeezing until he felt the bones start to creak.

Her eyes were closed and she was sucking her bottom lip, making a noise somewhere between a purr and a growl.

"Let's get the fuck out of here."

Now, the knife dents, but doesn't break her skin as he traces a thin, bloodless red line down between her breasts, over her belly and onto her pale inner thigh.

"Do you want me to cut you?" he asks.

"No."

"But you would let me do it?"

"Yes."

"Why?"

"I don't know."

They can still hear the juke joint right up on the hill—no music or melody, just the erratic pulse of bass thumping. All her clothes are in a heap on his floorboard.

An ounce more pressure and a drop of blood rises like an illusion on her skin. It appears violet in the blue glare of the headlights reflecting off the chrome grill. He touches his tongue to the drop and it burns through the taste of two-dollar whiskey.

She's a witch woman. If he doubted it before, he doesn't anymore.

Lightning flashes out in the desert and the mountains look like they're on the advance.

"Tell me what you want," he demands but she says nothing, just lies there, with her legs spread in mock invitation, tugging on the gold rings through her nipples.

"Roll over."

She slides forward on the hood until her bare feet are flat on the rocks. She looks at him and her eyes are the silver blue and black of gun barrels. She pirouettes and leans across the hood with the tips of her fingers stretched nearly to the windshield. Her ass is pointing toward him and it isn't perfect but it's close enough. On her right shoulder is a sunshine tattoo with some other guy's initials already inside. She still has traces of his skin underneath her nails.

He lays his hands flat on her back and feels the steady

vibration of the engine running through her like all of her secrets are humming from her skin. His hands burn and the palms feel etched with electricity. He runs them flat down her spine and she says, "You want to hurt me don't you?"

He doesn't answer so she says, "Do me with your belt."

Her words hit the back of his skull like chunks of hail and he drops the knife in the gravel at their feet. The thunder is rolling, the storm all around them and inside their skin.

"I won't," he tries to tell her. Even though he has no idea what he won't do. It doesn't matter, because he can already hear the leather clearing his belt loops, feel it wrapping around his fist once and then again. He holds himself still, muscles coiled and buzzing because he doesn't want to play her game. He hasn't figured out yet which of them is supposed to hurt.

When he cracks the belt, it pops a quarter inch above her skin, displacing air like a butterfly's wings. He catches his breath in his teeth and holds it tight. His cock is huge, a brand against his belly, and he rocks back a little on his feet.

He coils the belt up again and lets it loose, laying down a broad red stripe from her shoulder to the crack of her ass.

She shudders and sighs and the headlights throw rainbows off the juice running down her thighs.

"Again," she says and, "please."

She is trembling, her fingers tapping on the hood, chipping up his paint.

His jeans are bursting at the seams. He can feel the teeth of his zipper digging into his own sorry flesh.

He pulls back his arm, ready this time to really put something into the blow. He's got a lot of rage and pain just going to waste here.

As the leather whips forward, she rolls to the side like some sort of naked ninja and her feet are on his shoulders, her big toe pressed against his ear, a silver ring glittering on the baby one.

She's grinning and he sees a murder in her smile. Who's going to die here he doesn't care to guess.

The belt slaps the hood, but Detroit steel doesn't bend so easy and she laughs out loud as the rain starts to fall.

Her hands are working his buttons. She's going for his skin. But then she stops and takes his hand instead. She brings it to her face and uses his fingers to brush a damp curl from her forehead, moves him down her cheek and lays his palm against her throat. He can feel her pulse and his in his thumb but there's no way to know which is which.

"Nobody knows where I am," she says. "You can do anything to me, anything at all and no one would ever know."

There are at least a dozen guys up in the joint who've been where he is and another dozen standing in line.

His hands tighten on her throat. He can feel tiny bones shifting.

His cigarettes are in his breast pocket and she takes one out and puts it between her lips, those shiny eyes never leaving his. He lets go of her throat and fumbles in the pockets of his too-tight jeans. Once the cig is lit, she takes a drag and hands it back to him. He pinches it between his thumb and index finger because he saw it done that way in a movie one time and thought it looked cool. He puts the cigarette in his mouth and tastes where she's tongued the filter. She puts her hand inside his fly and takes hold of his aching cock.

"It's nice, you know," she says.

"Thanks." Because how do you respond to that?

He would say more but he's concentrating on not shooting his load across the lacy blue veins of her wrist.

"You want to slip it in me don't you?"

"Well, yeah, if it's not too much trouble. I mean we're already here and all."

"Sure baby, anything you want."

She's rubbing the ball of her thumb over his swollen cock head. Her tiny fist is loosening and contracting around his shaft with the beat of his own heart.

"You can put it in my mouth." *Rub.* "In my pussy." *Rub.* "In my ass. I know some girls won't take it there, but I don't mind." *Rub.*

When the fuck did she get so chatty?

He takes her hand to stop her restless rubbing.

It's raining harder, the drops beading up there on the hood and he's losing his grip on her hip. She's got her hand on his dick stroking and he knows that she's thinking he's just another one of them, another horny fuck she can twist and pull and break. Maybe she's right, but it pisses him off anyway.

"Do you even know my name?" he asks.

"Yes."

"Say it."

But she says nothing.

He grabs her shoulders and hauls her forward, crushing her tits against his chest. He's got his fist tangled in her hair and he's dragging her head back, exposing her throat to his teeth.

"Say it. Say my damn name."

She's breathing it into his hair, his name low and hoarse like he's still choking her.

"Say it again."

She's saying it over and over.

"Again."

The rain is coming harder now, it's pouring down into their faces, warm and slightly greasy like some sacramental oil. His shirt is sticking to his skin.

He groans against her chest and his teeth find her flesh. As she slips him inside, his jaws come together and he tastes her blood again.

He's moving inside her with frenzied, punishing strokes but still she's yelling out his name, using it to call down the rain. The wind is whipping up now, tearing around their feet, throwing sand against the car. The rain is falling and they can't hear the juke joint on the hill anymore, maybe it's rolled on like a tumbleweed, maybe it was never there at all.

She's shredding his back with her nails, digging her heels into the bony part of his ass. And he wants to ask her if those other guys ever do her like this, if they ever make her eyes do that crazy sexy rolling thing like there's poetry etched on her optic nerve if only she could find the right angle to read it.

She's slamming her head against the hood and he slips a hand under her neck and crushes her in tight.

"This is it," he says. "You with me baby?"

He holds her still, his cock raw and burning, near to bursting inside of her. When she opens her eyes, the steel has softened to the silvery gray of sunlit water and her mascara has smudged prettily across her cheek. She puts her lips against his. It isn't a kiss but something else and she breathes out, taking him still deeper inside and he whispers her own name back to her.

When he lays her back on the hood of the car again he's careful to hold her head. He's slamming into her and the hood ornament is digging a hole in his thigh. The rain steams off his skin and she's saying something but he can't hear the words over the rolling thunder or the ocean sound of his own beating blood. When he comes, it feels like something inside him is tearing loose and whatever it is—poison or poetry—he wants to give it all to her. Bury it deep inside where she can't dig it out.

Her cunt is contracting all around him like it wants to swallow him whole. He can feel her orgasm rocking the shocks on the car and the paint is peeling up under her nails in long curly ribbons.

He's holding her tight, his cock slowly softening and slipping out. Their fingers are entwined and he's squeezing so hard, it's hurting them both.

"I catch you up in there again, we're going to have us a problem, you understand?"

She nods and he slaps her hard on the thigh leaving a large red palm print on her damp skin.

"You understand?"

"Yes, I understand."

She whispers his name again and then he's kneeling there in the dirt in front of his own car kissing her fingers. She's laughing and it's a beautiful sound and the rain is washing her clean.

FRUITS OF THE FOREST

Kristina Lloyd

The woodland edge was tangled with great loops of wild clematis, and underfoot lay another tangle of barbed wire and brambles. I was slightly drunk so I placed my feet carefully, tramping on barbs with thick-soled gardening boots, holding my dress high so it wouldn't get snagged.

Oh, follow me, I thought. *Please follow me.* I was horny from sunshine and wine, and from the way he'd ignored me from the moment I arrived. When he plays hard to get, I'm the easiest girl in town.

Behind me lay the community garden, a jungle of bean wigwams, tumbledown sheds, orange flares of nasturtium, and huge sleepy sunflowers on a slope of land by the old railway track. I glanced back and through the trees and could see people milling about, smoke from the barbecue rising above the greenery like mists from a primeval swamp.

No one was following, so I stumbled on, taking my time because I was eager to get caught. The forest floor crackled and snapped, and around me trees grew taller and thicker. I was hot and thirsty, and the filtered leafy sunlight was a highball tumbler of lime juice I couldn't drink. Birds twittered somewhere unseen, and I began to feel spooked and lonely. Perhaps I should have told someone where I was going. But no, he'd seen me leave, hadn't he? I'd thrown him my best flirty glance and he'd responded with a quick, tilted smile. Based on past experience, I'd say a smile like that means "I want to fuck you to high heaven." So why the delay? What was he doing? Grilling a burger?

I paused by some scrawny bushes to text him, thumbing in those three little words: *tight white pantie—*

But I didn't complete my message. A flurry of noise behind me made my heart shoot, and I spun around, phone falling to the ground as a body thumped up hard against mine. I didn't even get a chance to scream. A hand was clamped over my mouth before I'd barely drawn breath. The hand wore a black leather glove and the smell of it was strong beneath my nostrils: an animal scent with a hint of manufacture. It added a squalid urbanity to the forest aromas of earthiness, wood rot, foxes and wild garlic. That hand didn't belong here. It was cruel and cold, and it belonged to alleyways and authority.

At the time, however, I wasn't thinking this. I was fighting and clawing, squealing in protest and thinking, *What the fuck?*

Together, we stumbled down a rugged incline to a small clearing. My heart was going nineteen to the dozen, my breath rushing against the leather in a humid pump and suck.

"Don't scream," he warned gently, and his voice wasn't the one I'd been hoping for.

He backed me up against a tree, uncovering my mouth as he moved behind the trunk to catch at my wrists. I didn't scream. I just breathed hard and fast, glimpsing a skinny figure in jeans, trainers and a hooded top. A length of thin rope flicked in the corner of my eye—hemp twine from the garden—and then he was using it to tether my wrists behind the tree trunk. The bark was rough on my bare arms, and my skin was clammy. No, it wasn't who I was expecting, that's for sure.

He crouched at my feet where the ground was lumpy with roots and looped the cord above my chunky boot. A small backpack lay in front of us but that didn't give me much of a clue.

"Danny?" I asked, but got no reply. He was intent on securing me, bunny-hopping around the tree base with the rope. In the distance a bird cawed noisily, a jay or magpie. When it stopped, the silence was eerie. Something rustled in the undergrowth nearby. The man passed the rope behind the trunk then caught my other leg in another loop. His gloved hand brushed against my shins, and the touch of it lingered. Watching him work, I saw that he was being careful to shield his face, and those dark anonymous hands took on a life of their own. I could imagine them in all sorts of places: on the wheel of a car, in the pockets of a cashmere coat, on a coffin-bearer's hands, forcing the lock of a lamp-lit door. They were like puppets, dancing and disembodied.

His hands must have been hot. My feet certainly were. I wished I'd worn pretty sandals so my toes could breathe. But the garden terrain is tricky, and I like to be able to move about freely. Ironic, considering I was now tied to a tree.

From behind, the man reached around and let his leather fingers drift briefly over my face. I could hear him breathing from his exertions, and my own breath was choppy too.

"Mike?" I tried, and I heard him laugh. If this wasn't a man I knew, I was in big trouble.

He stepped out into the clearing, shucking off his zip-up top and stooping for his bag. Tall, angular, sinewy arms, faded black T-shirt, scruffy peroxide spikes and some serious cheekbones. "My god, Brett?! Is that right? Is that your name?"

He turned, grinning with sly confidence and scattering half glances in my direction. Stubble speckled his jaw, and his dark brows matched the dark deliberate roots peeping through the bleach. He looked as if he'd been up all night, half angel, half devil, a wasted, fucked-up pretty boy.

I glanced away. On the edge of the clearing, a haze of midges shimmered in sunlight. The tree trunk felt thick against my open thighs. The woodland was still and tranquil. Brett took a large margarine tub from his backpack and peeled off the top. Inside were raspberries. My mouth watered: pimply scarlet berries, fuzzed with hair, flecked with leaf, and lying several cushiony inches deep.

"I want to feed you," he said, stepping closer. "I've always wanted to feed you."

Lust thumped me open because I'd no idea that this man had wanted to *anything* me. I watched his black leather fingertips scoop up a little cluster of fruit. Thin juices bled from them as he stepped closer still, and a drip fell as he brought the berries to my mouth. I was so thirsty, and the raspberries crumbled on my tongue, a brush of fur popping to sharp wet sweetness and then, too quickly, they slid down my throat. The insides of my cheeks tingled.

"More," I said, and he fingered up another serving, hurrying them to my lips. Juice dribbled on my chin, and I snatched a suck on his leather fingers when they were deep in my mouth. God, what a combination. Flavors burst, and it all tasted of summer and peaty bonfires with the slightest tang of licorice and metal. Those berries couldn't get any riper. They were at their limit, on the edge of decay and close to collapse.

So was I. Brett. I hardly knew him. A friend of a friend, a man I'd probably chatted to once or twice while privately admiring his cheekbones. He'd been at the barbecue but we hadn't even said "Hi." And here he was, ladling raspberries into my mouth, allowing me to suck on his leather gloves as if tart sweet fluid might ooze from his fingers.

Before I could swallow, he pressed more raspberries into my mouth then squashed several onto the flat of my chest, rubbing with his gloved hand. Cool juice trickled toward my cleavage, and my skin was smeared with smashed fruit.

"Don't waste them," I said, pulling against my ropes and opening wide for more.

"Not going to," he replied, and he set down the punnet and lifted the hem of my dress.

He twisted the fabric tight, wringing it into a tail that he tucked behind me, leaving me exposed from the waist downward. He stooped for more raspberries, then, pulling the elastic, he slid his hand into those tight white panties and crushed soft red berries into my cunt. His leather fingers paddled and probed, mashing me and the fruit into one glorious pulpy crimson mess.

I groaned, wanting to slide down the tree in mindless, soporific lust. He took more berries, pushing them higher into me this time, his hard, leathered fingers stirring in my hole. I felt like I was part of a recipe: *insert fruit and mix well.* Around us, trees whispered in the breeze, a bee buzzed somewhere at ground level, and I could feel my face flushing with shame and arousal.

Brett watched me, his blue-gray eyes shy and fascinated. "Is it good?" he smiled, fingers still working.

I could barely speak. "Fuck, yes," I breathed. "So good...it's so good."

As I moved, the bark scoured the backs of my thighs and arms, and the twine rubbed my wrists and shins. But I couldn't keep still. Brett's fingers squirmed. *I* squirmed. He shuffled closer, resting his free hand against the trunk and leaning toward my mouth. A glint of sunlight sparked on his dark lashes and his breath was warm against my skin. Carefully, he took my lower lip between his teeth, pulling ever so gently. He repeated the action, teeth lightly scraping and all the while his gloved hand kept churning between my thighs. I whimpered, trying to kiss him back, but he dodged my mouth, smearing kisses over my face instead, bristles scratching.

His words blurred against my skin. "I've always wanted to feed you. Feed you. And feed me." Kiss, kiss, went his lips. "Here. Try."

He withdrew his hand from me and brought it up to my mouth. The glove was hot and moist, and he held a finger sidelong to my lips. I licked through my fast-rushing breath, and so did he. I tasted myself, all mixed up with raspberries and leather. And I tasted him, the quick lash of his tongue and his cool, clean saliva. Between my thighs, I was hot and syrupy, damp white cotton holding a pouch of pulped raspberries. He rubbed me there, and his breath tickled my ear as he murmured, "And now I'm going to gobble you up."

My head spun as he dropped to his knees. Leather fingers brushed my thighs and he pulled down my underwear as far as it would go. I strained against my bondage, thrusting forward, hips trying to seek him out. For a moment, the forest air breezed against my bared pussy and then his mouth was on me, hot, sodden and writhing.

I moaned loudly, the sound seeming to shock the clearing where only birds and bees made noises. He gulped me down, tongue and lips searching out fruit and flesh. My clit was a raspberry that wouldn't dissolve but he tried his damnedest, licking, sucking, flicking, rocking. His hands made sticky prints on my thighs where he gripped me, and he nuzzled deep, all greedy, slurpy and shameless. When he drove those strong leather fingers up inside me, I came hard, spilling fruit and nectar into his hungry, wolfish throat.

The trees whirled in a haze of sunny greens, my body clenched, my cunt melted and the bees just kept on bumbling and buzzing.

Brett stood, his chin and mouth glistening with pinkish stains and crimson gobbets. He looked like he'd been feeding at a trough. He wiped the back of his hand across his mouth and grinned.

"One day…" he said, looking more satisfied than perhaps he ought. He nodded in the direction we'd both come from. Somewhere beyond the woods there was a party going on. "I've got to get back," he said, slinging his bag onto his shoulder.

"What about me?" I said, but he was already off, scrambling up the slope he'd dragged me down not long ago.

Was he going to leave me here? Pinned open like a butterfly, gummy, half-naked and defenseless against wasps?

"Hey!" I shouted.

He paused at the top of the slope, casting around on the forest floor.

"My phone!" I hollered, remembering that I'd dropped it. He'd obviously remembered too because he pounced for it before my words were finished. I could see him looking at the screen, and I recalled my text: *tight white pantie—*

"*s!*" I called. "Needs an *s* on the end!"

He pressed a button.

"Is it for Tom?" he asked.

"Well, who else?" I replied.

He thumbed a few buttons and, from the smile on his face, I could tell the text was sent.

He tossed the phone to the ground. "If I pass him en route," he said, walking away, "I'll tell him where you are."

I struggled against my ropes. "Strawberries!" I yelled. "Tell him to bring strawberries!"

He turned to grin and I knew, without a doubt, that the two men would pass.

NERVOUS BOY

Xan West

He is nervous. He almost didn't make it out the door. He stands on the corner of Nineteenth and Lexington, eyes darting as he chain-smokes in the cold.

He can't believe he is here. His boots carried him here against his will, his hunger outweighing his anxiety. It was pure ache that motivated his post; a nervous, bold naming of his desire: cocky little scared boy aching to fuck drunkenly. He needs the alcohol to hide from his own self. And I have forbidden it, which really pisses him off.

How can I demand he meet me at a bar and then require him to be sober?

It's the anger that motivates him to walk into the bar. He stands at the far wall, staring, heart racing. He can't do this.

He is curiously near to the bar and his hand jams into his pocket to see how many drinks he could get. His chin sticks out, he's thinking he could just sit here all night, drinking, watching me as I sit quietly at the table, writing. He could down his tequila and watch my boots as I leave, never approaching me.

He catches a glimpse of my eyes as I glance up in his direction. Unbidden, an image fills his head, my eyes looking down at him as I force his head down onto my cock. He tries to shake it off, but it keeps coming.

It's this image that motivates his boots to cross the floor to me without his full permission. I have paused in my writing to watch the floor by my feet, checking for a nervous boy's approach. Which is a good thing, otherwise I would not have heard the throaty, tentative, "Sir?" And who knows if he would have the guts to repeat it.

I lift my head to look him over, noticing his dusty boots, the bulge in his torn jeans, his pecs bound down so he passes better, his twitching hands, the pulse in his throat racing. I meet his eyes, and nod to the chair across from me.

"I have two questions for you, boy."

His eyes dart from my lips to the floor.

"Are you sober?"

"Yes," he says grumpily.

I nod acknowledging that I believe him.

"What is your safeword?"

His eyes widen with fear. He swallows, speaking softly, "Red."

"Very good. Carry my bag, boy." I gesture to it, shrugging on my jacket and striding out of the bar, knowing he will follow.

I had described to him what I was going to do to him, and he racks his brain trying to remember exactly what I had written. All he can think about is that image of my eyes meeting his, my cock deep in his throat. His heart is racing and he is struggling to keep up with my long strides, his eyes focused on my boots.

I hear his frantic pace behind me, confirming my trust, and turn the corner, stalking to the spot. I stand against the wall, knowing I need to keep one eye on the street. I watch his nervous eyes, his boots shuffling, the pulse beating in his throat, and a surge of power fills me. I breathe it in deep and feel it lift me, my cock throbbing. In these moments I am not conscious of the fact that my cock is attached by thin strips of leather. It is fully mine, and the throbbing is very real.

My gloved hand moves steadily toward his face, knowing his eyes are mesmerized by it. It rests briefly against his cheek, and he breathes the scent of leather before he feels it grip him, thumb stroking his throat as the gloved hand presses against the back of his neck.

His heart leaps to his throat and I can feel it race against my thumb. *It's not fair*, his mind screams. He wordlessly drops to his knees and looks up.

There is nothing like the first sight of a boy on his knees. I rake over him with my eyes, taking my time. My thumb strokes the pulse of his throat, claiming him. He is mine, under my hand, in my care; if only for the duration of this scene, he is mine. There's the thrill of reading him, watching his responses, carefully deciding how to play with him. I can taste my own fear in my mouth—will I be able to read him? There have been so few words between us. Can I read his body, his energy? The fear only ups the ante. I sink into my self-trust, planting my feet in it. The back of my hand strokes his cheek. My thumb grazes his lips.

I watch him carefully as I free my cock. His eyes widen. Is that fear? Excitement? Both, I decide, stroking my cock as I watch him. He is scared—what if it isn't how he wanted? Or worse, what if it is? What if he really is a cocksucking fagboy who gets on his knees for strangers in alleys?

"You want this, don't you?"

His eyes widen further. He licks his lips in silent response. My cock swells as I speak softly to him, stroking.

"You've been dreaming about this, haven't you? This is what

you crave, being on your knees in an alley, a cock in front of your lips. You are aching to have my dick in your throat."

His heart hammers in his head. He is so still, afraid that if he moves he will run. And he doesn't want to run. This is where he wants to be. In an alley. On his knees.

His lips part. He can't stop staring at my cock. My hand cups the back of his head, twisted in his hair. This is the moment. The moment when he needs to own his desire.

My hand gently pulls his head toward my cock. It is centimeters from his lips. But he must close the distance. He must choose this. One movement is enough and then there will be no more choices.

Time is suspended. His eyes reach up for me, begging me to force him. Fear rushes through his body in waves and I soak it all in, sourcing power from it through my hand at the back of his head.

My smile softens just a bit. "Put your mouth on it, boy. Wrap your lips around my cock." And I am softly stroking his hair, drawing off the shame. "My cock is throbbing, aching for your mouth, boy."

The tenderness in my voice and my gestures opens up a rawness he can feel in his chest. It scares him. And seduces him. He wants to be this naked, this vulnerable. He wants to be this cared for, this claimed. He wants to please me. This is a good place to be, on his knees in an alley about to suck my cock. This is where he belongs, who he is. His mouth eagerly moves to engulf my cock, his eyes on mine, offering. I meet his gaze, allowing some cruelty to slide into my smile.

I grip his head, and we start the ride. My cock ravaging every inch. Relentless. Claiming his throat, in achingly full strokes.

He had that moment of choice, but this is *my* moment. My moment to wring every ounce of pleasure out of his mouth and

throat. He is mine for this glorious moment. Made for my pleasure. My mouth to fuck. My throat to use.

I growl, my hand twisting his hair as I thrust into his throat,
watching him gag, grinning at the tears in his eyes. I am fucking him, filling him, powerful and relentless in my possession of
him. And then I encircle him with my words.

"Yes, boy. I love fucking your throat, claiming it. Give it to
me. Let me take it all. This is what you crave. This is what you
ache for. Being on your knees. Sucking off a stranger in an alley.
My fagboy. My cocksucker. That's who you are. A cocksucker
born to please me. Your mouth was made for my cock."

I thrust deep, watching his eyes, and the truth washes into
him and over him through his throat and his ears, and his eyes
spill over as that raw place inside him is opened and filled with
my cock and his desire and my cruelty and his tears and my relentless tenderness.

He is sobbing around my cock as I ruthlessly fuck his throat.
The sight of his tears draws my cream in long spurts that rack
my body as the guttural growl from my throat wraps into the
sounds of his sobs. He swallows every drop, taking it down and
absorbing it. His eyes lift and ache for mine. I reach down and
stroke his cheek, saying gruffly, "Good boy."

I smile down at him, ease out of his mouth and hug him to
me. He reaches up and holds on, soaking in who he is, a boy on
his knees, held by the man standing over him, the man he just
pleased. Proud.

We are still. But not for long. I start feeling an itch in my
hands, an ache in my belly. I want more. I look down at him,
tilting his chin up to meet my eyes.

"Grab my bag, boy."

I pull him into a cab. "Mission and Van Ness," I tell the driver. My hand is resting on the back of his neck, stroking gently.

It's not long before I'm pulling him into the club, and heading downstairs. I drag him to the side of the room right by the door. The fence demarcates this space for voyeurs. And I hope there will be voyeurs. I want to feed off the crowd. Pull their energy into me for use. I want this witnessed. There is a bench. And a wall. And a quiet bondage scene nearby.

I slowly push him backward into the wall, crowding him, my hands on either sides of his head, my breath moving his hair. I take in the smell of him. I drop closer and breathe him in. I can feel his pulse speed up against my cheek. His sweat has a metallic scent to it. He is afraid.

I step back and meet his eyes, hardening my gaze. There will be no coaxing here. This is about strength. *His*. And will. *Mine*. I am building something very important. I sink into my boots and begin.

I slam him into the wall, glorying in the feel of his body against mine. Again. The breath is thrust out of him. Again. The sound of flesh against concrete. Again.

I turn around, lean my back against him, and grab my SAP gloves. I tease his face with them, let him feel the leather against his lips, his jaw, his throat. The lead shot drives into him. I am tapping him lightly, but it does not feel light. Stepping up the intensity, I can feel his energy shift as he realizes I am barely using my strength. The back of my neck prickles and I can sense people behind me. I focus my hearing and I pick out whispering, feet shuffling, breath quickening. A crowd is starting to build.

I begin to pound into him with my fists. I am getting at the deep muscles now. His chin is lifting higher. I watch his eyes and realize that I have found his stubborn streak. It's time.

"Show me how strong you are, boy. Show me how much you can take."

I slam into him, taking his breath, scenting him. There is

something sweet there, now. It's not just fear I smell. I step back and drive my knee into his cock. He gasps, and struggles to stay still. Again. I can see the steel in his eyes. Good.

Now to really get started. I step back further, and start pounding my boots into his thighs. He is breathing audibly now. I am gliding around him. Slamming into him with punches. Ramming my weight into him. Thudding kicks into his thighs. The energy builds as the crowd builds. There is a rawness to this that draws them in.

"Come on, boy. You can take it. I know you're strong enough."

I drive my boot heel into the bruises on his thigh. I ram my elbow into the bruises on his pecs. He grunts, clenching his jaw. He's not sure he can do it, but he'll never admit it.

"Yes, Sir, I can take it," he spits out, glaring at me, promising himself as much as me.

I build him up with punches and kicks. Show him I can see his strength by how hard I pound into him. My face is full of ferocity and pride and I pour all that into him, until it streams out in tears running down his face.

I don't stop there. He deserves nothing less than the full force of my will. I can feel the energy building again and I grab him by the neck and bend him over the bench, yanking his pants to his knees. Slowly, I take off my belt, knowing his ears are attuned to the sound of the buckle being released, of leather pulled through denim. I fold the belt in half, twice, and snap it, watching him twitch.

The leather bites into him. The belt brings me to a ravenous place. I want to open him up. I want to rip him apart. I want to be inside him. I never take out my belt unless I'm sure I'm going to fuck, because it does this to me every time.

"Take it, boy. That's right. Scream for me. I know you can do it. Show me how strong you can be."

Each hit ramps it up. Each welt a badge of strength. He rides on it, grounded in pride, sure of himself now. I growl as I concentrate on one spot. I want to ram into him so hard. I claim him with the belt instead, striking out with the bite of it, waiting for the moment when I allow myself to fuck him. We both grunt with the last blow.

I pull out my cock, slide on the condom and lube it up. I can't wait any longer. I pull down his boxers and ready my cock at his ass. I push in slowly, making room for myself inside him. He is so tight it makes me groan. I keep pushing, and his muscles slowly relax as he lets me in deeper.

"Take it, boy. That's it. Take it all."

And he does. Until I'm buried inside him, throbbing. I set my teeth into his shoulder and bite down. And then I start to move, rotating my hips, grinding my invasion into him with teeth and cock. I lift my head and whisper into his ear. "I'm so proud of you, boy." And then I start to fuck him. Driving into him with my cock, just as relentless as before. "Take it for me, boy. That's it. Take my dick in your ass."

He is whimpering, as my weight presses into his welts. I rub my face into his sweat as I fuck him, burning him with my stubble. He smells delicious, and I thrust my teeth into his neck. And then he is coming, and sobbing, and screaming. His sounds reach inside and milk my cock. I growl as I spurt into his ass. "Good boy. I'm proud of you. You have pleased me very much."

I slip out of him, pull him up, and slowly lick the tears from his cheeks. I capture his eyes and motion him to my boots. He kneels gratefully and looks up at me, eyes pleading. I nod, and push his head down to my boot, one heel on the back of his neck.

"You earned it, boy," I say gruffly, and groan as I feel his tongue on my boot.

I settle in, with my back against the wall and his mouth on my boot. Content.

SHE LOOKED GOOD IN RIBBONS

Sommer Marsden

West stuck his hand in his jacket pocket, rubbed the paper, removed his hand. He shook his head at himself. He was going to rub a hole in the fucking paper if he kept rubbing it like a worry stone.

"Here you go, Mr. Harper."

"West," he corrected the desk manager.

The man frowned. "We have you down as Westbrook Harper. That isn't right?"

West stifled a sigh. "It is, but I'm here for the convention and...we're supposed to check in under our...working names."

The man, whose name tag read, BLAKE, immediately flushed. "Of course, Mr. West. I do apologize. I am normally more discreet but the sudden flood of check-ins has me off my game."

West nodded and shrugged. "It's fine." While he waited for his key, he found his hand returning to his pocket. He was crazy. Certifiable. He should throw out the paper and go back to the airport. Return to normal life. Let this go.

But he wouldn't.

"...anything else?"

West glanced up at the man's annoyed expression. He'd been off in space again. Way down deep in his own mind where he could barely hear the outside world around him. He cleared his throat. "I'm sorry?"

"Your key." He slid the key across the marble counter. "Was there anything else, Mr. West?"

He had to clear his throat again and still his voice was slow to come. "Alyssa? What room is she in?"

Tapping on the keys and keeping a neutral expression, Blake checked. "I see here permission from Ms. Alyssa to tell you... Room Two-Thirteen."

At the word *permission,* West felt himself go a little weak in the knees. She had made arrangements for him to know her room number. "Thank you," he managed.

"The dinner will be in the Ballroom at seven, Mr. West."

West nodded and practically fled to the bank of elevators. When he stepped in and hit the number two button, he realized his other hand was in his fucking pocket again. He was alone, so he gave in to the urge and unfolded the badly creased paper.

> W,
>
> *It's not that I want to be trussed up like a turkey or anything. The whole idea of being bound some-how and at someone's mercy (kind mercy, mind you) is thrilling. I guess it shows up in my work quite of-ten. Is there such a thing as soft bondage, I wonder? Ah well, work to do. I have become way too wrapped up in your emails. You're addictive.*
>
> *Alyssa*
>
> *P.S. Hope you can work out the trip to the confer-*

*ence. I can't imagine meeting all those erotic artists
and not meeting you. You're my favorite after all....*

So he had worked it out. Fought with his wife. Spent the money.
All to meet this woman who seemed so much like him. *He* was
addictive? That always stumped him. He was a normal man who
did normal things. He just happened to be an artist whenever
time would allow and sex had always been his favorite subject.
So much to explore. So much inspiration. She did the same. And
she was addictive. And he was on the second floor.

He stood outside the elevator, refolded the email, shoved it
deep into his pocket. He checked the other pocket and heard
the cellophane protest at his brutal squeeze. He pulled out the
packet and checked them again. This whole damn thing was
making him borderline obsessive compulsive. Checking and re-
checking everything because if he didn't, this wouldn't turn out
as it was supposed to. The fantasy would become a hideous fi-
asco he would carry with him forever. He let out the breath he
had been holding. They were all there. Five ribbons: hot pink,
turquoise, lime green, sunshine yellow, and red. Pilfered from his
wife's craft closet. *You sick bastard...* He ignored the thought,
closed his eyes, called up the use for these ribbons he had been
imagining for weeks. Sifted them through his fingers.

"Soft bondage," he whispered. Then he put them away. He
turned left for 213 and prayed he wasn't fucking up his whole life.

She opened the door, looking twice as nervous as he felt. It didn't
affect what he saw when he looked at her. Nothing like he had
imagined. Then again, he wasn't so sure what he had imagined.

Her blonde hair was the color of sunlight on water. It was
cut into a short bob that reminded him of a flapper. Strands
brushed her jawline as she bowed her head and peered at him

from behind the shield of her hair. Her eyes were what stopped his breath, though. She was tall, so he was looking dead into them and for just a second he fought for air as if he were drowning. They were the color of a sky right before the storm comes, flecked with a true blue. Around the pupils, a fairy ring of green accented the shades of blue.

"Do you want to come in?" she asked, looking more nervous under his gaze. He realized she probably thought he was disappointed or having second thoughts when in fact he was simply stunned.

"I'm married," he said. A hell of an introduction, West thought. Stupid. She already knew that.

"Me, too," she sighed but then stepped back for him to enter. So he entered.

She sat on the bed and smiled. "I feel like I should shake your hand or something. Hug you? Would that be weird?"

"It's all weird," he sighed but smiled.

When she offered her hand, he took it. Shook it. Turned it in his larger hand and studied her palm. The creases there. The paint stains on her fingers. Long, thin fingers with perfectly shaped nails. He loved her hands and what they were capable of. He had seen her work but had never expected her to be as breathtaking as the images she created.

"We don't have to do anything," she said. Her head was still bowed but her hand twisted in his. "We can pretend that we came here to meet and network. We can pretend that we had no intention of living out any of the things we discussed...."

When she said that, his skin felt two sizes too small and his lungs refused to draw air. Her confirmation of their intentions, the fact that she had thought the same things despite the fact that neither had put the words down on the screen, was intensely arousing. West sucked in a breath and held it, stabilizing his heart rate. He steeled himself for denial and then spoke, "I want to tie you up, Alyssa."

For just a second the words hung there, suspended in the air, not fading or falling to earth. They hovered. And he watched her.

Her eyes grew wide and it was if he had touched her. Her cheeks flushed to a deep pink, her full lips parted and she actually shifted on the bed. Squirmed. It was if his words had made her wet. Just the thought was enough to make his cock jerk to life and his heart beat wildly.

West had his answer. The one he had obsessed over for countless hours. Lost sleep over. Daydreamed about. The answer he wanted more than he wanted to breathe at the moment. He took in the room. The headboard was a solid hunk of wood, carved and trimmed in gold. No good. His eyes roamed.

She must have been reading his mind because she caught his gaze and said softly, "In the sitting room. It's perfect."

West left her on the bed. He took a moment and touched his jacket pocket, hearing the reassuring and suddenly erotic sound of the cellophane bag. He walked through the doorway and surveyed the tiny room. Alyssa was right, it was perfect. A bentwood rocker. It was a beautiful piece of furniture but the many curves and elaborate scrollwork were what drew his attention.

He went back to get Alyssa.

He didn't say anything as he undressed her. He liked hearing the soft little sounds that escaped her when his hands brushed her naked belly. Naked thighs. Breasts. When he tweaked one dusky nipple and it beaded under his fingers, he started doing math in his head to tame his urge to simply sink into her heat without preamble. Her responses, how much she clearly wanted him had him half insane.

Alyssa remained quiet but he felt her studying him. Felt her gaze skitter over his skin, warming him as she watched. She watched everything he did. Even when he closed his eyes to steady himself, he felt her staring.

"I want you to sit now. You're ready? No second thoughts?"

She shook her head, sat, smiled. *Ready,* her actions practically screamed in the silent room. West felt a giant weight fly from him. She understood him. It was something that he was missing so severely lately. He was tired of the arguments with his wife about his work. Tired of hearing about the time it stole from "them." Tired of the insinuations that he was simply a pervert and nothing more. *Your porn paintings* is what she called his work. Sometimes, West just wanted to grab her and shake her and shout in her face. *You said you understood me. Now I think you lied.* But he didn't and he wouldn't.

"West?"

He snapped back to her, drank her in. How open her face was. Kind, understanding, patient, excited. It was all there and he felt himself grow harder than he thought he could. So he took the bag from his pocket and he pulled the ribbons out one by one. Her eyes followed them. Tracked the slide of each brightly colored ribbon as he tugged it.

"Oh," she sighed.

"Soft bondage," he said, reminding her in case she had forgotten. He knew she hadn't.

Without him asking, she parted her thighs, placing each delicate ankle by the shaped curves of wood near the bottom of the rocker. He started with turquoise. Blue like her eyes. He kissed her knees and then slid the ribbon around her ankles, through the scrollwork, over the wood. Tied the ribbon slowly. He pulled out the green one, looped it under one curvy thigh and slid it through the side of the rocker. Took his time and tied it. The pink cradled her other thigh and secured her. The yellow ribbon he draped across the back of her neck. He let it hang down between her breasts, the slightly frayed ends brushing the very tops of her thighs.

"Put your hands out," he said, running the wide red ribbon through his fingers.

They sprang out instantly and her chest rose and fell swiftly with frenzied breath. West heard himself moan softly. He wasn't sure he'd actually have to touch her to get off. She was that perfect. That here. Right here with him and nothing was occupying her mind but what they were doing. He wound the ribbon around her wrists several times, pulling it tight enough that she gasped just a little. He wanted to make sure that Alyssa got what she wanted—what she needed—from him. West wanted to give her everything, anything she wanted.

He stared at the red encircling her wrists, binding them together. How her hands looked as if folded in prayer. It was the most erotic image he had ever seen. It embodied everything he wanted from her: trust, obedience, attention...love?

"Done," he whispered and then stepped back to study her. She met his gaze and smiled, her eyes all shiny and full of hope. Full of arousal. The blue startling and vivid. He shut his eyes and memorized the look of her pale skin wrapped in the vibrant ribbons. He would paint her. There wasn't any way he could *not* paint her.

He took his time removing his clothes. Piece by piece he folded them, setting them on the loveseat behind him. He gave her time to watch him. Time to change her mind or come to her senses. When he turned she smiled again. The same eagerness evident on her face and god help him, she licked her lips. His cock jumped in response and her eyes grew even brighter. So West took the yellow ribbon in his hands.

His cock slid between her lips effortlessly. She parted for him, taking him in, like his wife never had before. Like no one ever had before. She had been waiting for this and he could tell. The feel of him, the taste of him on her lips was something she had considered many times before. The truth of this set West free. He pushed beyond the barrier or her teeth, felt her soft tongue on his erection, fucked her mouth. He was free. Lulled by the feel of the hot suede of her mouth rushing to encompass him as he gently pushed the rocker back and forth, back and forth. A metronome of pleasure. The universe boiled down to one bright point in his mind—her mouth on him.

She looked up at him with her eyes wide open, hair swinging gently against her jaw from him rocking her. He felt it building within him, an orgasm he had thought about for too many days to count. He withdrew, feeling a brief stab of melancholy at the loss of her moisture. He pushed the feeling away and knelt before her. He feathered his hands over her skin, and felt nearly out of his mind when her skin pebbled beneath his touch. She wanted him. That fact was almost too much for him to bear.

His fingers sought her out instantly. How wet she was startled him for just a moment. How easy it was to sink first one and then a second finger deep inside of her. Fascinated, he watched as they disappeared within her, sinking to the hilt. He moved them, pushing deeper, forcing them against her, watching her face so he could see each flicker of pleasure. He grabbed the yellow ribbon again and pulled her forward, tilting the rocker to his advantage. He kissed her. Her mouth opened for him as easily as her body had. She pushed her tongue against his, devouring his mouth with hers. The inside of her mouth was as hot and moist as the inside of her cunt.

Alyssa moaned into his mouth and the sound mixed with the vibration made his body short-circuit and suddenly he could think of nothing but driving into her. Making her body open for his. The sweetest invasion he could think of.

He didn't release the yellow ribbon, though it cut into the soft skin of her slender throat. Seeing her body tilt toward his as he led her by her neck was enough to make his blood sing in his veins.

"Scoot forward. Toward me. As much as the ribbons will let you," he managed. His voice sounded primitive to his own ears. Unrecognizable. An animalistic growl buried under the words.

Alyssa did. Wriggled in the caned seat. She moved toward him, her knees falling open even further, her cunt opening to him. He parted her, tried to tattoo the image of her swollen sex in his mind. He kissed the small bud of her clit. Allowed himself the pleasure of suckling her there. Tasting her. The little cry that escaped her reminded him that he had to be in her.

Kneeling between her knees, he pushed into her. No finesse. No patience. Just pushed into her. He buried himself in her and she cried out softly near his ear as he tugged the yellow ribbon. Her arms came around his neck, a bright flash of red in his peripheral vision. The red ribbon bound her in prayer. Prayer that this would one day actually happen; and he moved faster, deeper inside of her. His mind shut down. His body took over. His ears buzzed as he looked at her. Her face was a mask of pleasure even as tears slipped from behind her closed lids. She looked like a woman who had found something she thought was lost to her forever.

He pulled the yellow ribbon. Thought of the red one behind his head, trapping her hands together just for him. At his mercy. *Kind* mercy. Pulling the yellow ribbon, he moved her faster toward him. Driving himself harder against her. He felt her cunt clench around his cock, felt her muscles as they galloped around him.

"Oh," she sighed again, and that one word spoke volumes as she came.

It did him in. He gave the yellow ribbon one final yank and heard himself nearly sob as he came inside her welcoming heat. Then he let himself fall on her. Let his skin rest on her skin. He knew she was crying. Hell, he felt like crying himself.

Her arms were still looped around his neck. The red ribbon tickled the middle of his back. It made him shiver. West kissed her forearm. Ran his tongue over the skin. Tasted the salty sweet tang of her.

"We have two days," she said almost shyly.

"We do," he agreed.

He started to untie her but he did it slowly. Not quite ready to give this up yet. He knew he would have to return the ribbons to his wife's stuff. Not the red one, though. He would find someplace safe to keep it. Maybe in the part of the garage he used as a studio. Keep it safe. Keep it close.

BLINDED

Donna George Storey

I kneel down and he ties the blindfold over my eyes.

Strictly speaking, it isn't a blindfold, it's a silk scarf. My brother and his wife gave it to me for Christmas, a pretty thing with a floral design in crimson, deep blue and gold. But when I opened the gift, I was thinking: *When will I ever wear* this?

But I gave it a try. When we got home, I spent a good fifteen minutes in front of the mirror attempting to tie it into an appealing fashion accessory. He sat on the edge of the bed and watched smugly—my brother had gotten *him* some Charlie Parker CDs.

Then I got the idea to wear the scarf as a headband, to keep my bangs off my face. Another failure.

"I can't do anything with this thing. I'm sure it was expensive, too. Do you think they'd get mad if I took it back?"

He walked over to me. "How about this way?" He pulled the bottom edge of the scarf down over my eyes.

I could still see him hazily through the single layer of loose silk. He looked at me for a moment, his head tilted to one side as if he were deciding what to do. Then he kissed me. Hard.

When we finally came up for air, my lips felt tender, a little swollen.

I said, "Now tie it on so I can't see."

That was the beginning. I've lost count of how many times we've done it since then, but it's gotten us through this long winter. Sometimes he blindfolds me. Sometimes I blindfold him. It all depends on who comes up with a new idea. It's never the same. That's our unspoken rule.

Not that it's entirely unpredictable. He seems to prefer that I wear some sort of clothing: one of his shirts or a teddy, something he can eventually slip off. After more than a year together, it still excites him to uncover my breasts, weigh them in his hands as if he is touching them for the first time. That's one of the things I like about him.

I prefer him to be completely naked. The first time I blindfolded him, I was the one who was trembling. Although it was my idea that he kneel on the bed wearing nothing but the blindfold, when he actually began to undress with a cool smile, I almost told him to stop. I wasn't sure I really wanted to see his big body so exposed, a band of flowered silk over his eyes with the long, loose ends falling softly down his back. I thought it might somehow diminish him.

But I was wrong. I'd never realized how beautiful his body was. Not that I hadn't appreciated it before, but I'd always focused my gaze on his eyes, his expressions. The rest of him I knew better by touch. But now, with his eyes hidden, I could see him with a new clarity: the rich, taut curves of his arms and chest, the hint of soft flesh at his waist that I found oddly pleasing. I noticed that the hair on his belly fanned out more luxuriantly to the left, and by contrast, his right thigh was slightly more muscular, a legacy of his college fencing days. It didn't take long for him to get hard—it never did when we used the blindfold—and I got to watch that, the delicate jerking movements of his penis as it rose and thickened, drawn upward by invisible puppet strings which, I imagined, led straight to my hands.

I felt like a thief.

I felt my own desire grow within me in a completely new way. This time, the familiar ache seemed to originate from behind my eyes, from the very sight of him unseeing. Then it seeped downward, bringing a warm flush to my cheeks and neck, making my nipples grow erect. It finally reached my belly, pooling there as a sharp, shimmering hunger.

I bent closer to feast, on the smell of him first, sharply male, yet intimate, intoxicating. I'd never studied a cock so carefully, the web of tiny veins embedded in the skin like red lace, the puckered ridge below the head, as if the flesh had been pinched when it was still fresh and soft. With no eyes glowing down at me, urging me to lick and suck and swallow, I could gaze into that other eye, slit vertically like a cat's, or maybe more like a tiny, hairless cunt, what they'd have on Barbie if she were anatomically correct. I pressed my tongue against it, lightly, tasting bitterness and salt, the tang of soap, then took the whole smooth helmet of the head into my mouth.

He moaned.

At last I had the sound of him.

Music.

When he decides the game, he often feeds me things. A dish of rice pudding in baby-sized bites from a spoon. Morsels of praline truffle he pushes through my lips with his tongue. And most often, his cock. I don't know why, but his semen tastes sweeter when I am wearing the blindfold.

One time he slipped a tiny wedge of soft paper between my lips, struck a match, and instructed me to inhale. It was a joint. *Where did you get this?* I wanted to ask, but I knew I wasn't supposed to talk—he had a way of letting me know such things—so I just lay quietly next to him on the bed and took long drags whenever he held it to my mouth. It must have been good stuff, because soon I was tingling all over just this side of numbness, floating off the bed into the past. It had been years since I'd smoked a joint. I never bought drugs myself. They were always presented to me as an offering from a boy in exchange for what I could offer him in return. So many things had changed since then, but it took me back to a time when I was so dumb about men, I might as well have been wearing a scarf over my eyes.

It's been a difficult winter for both of us. I know things aren't going well for him at work, but I didn't realize how upset he was until that day when I came home to find him practicing with his saber.

Once, when we first started going out, he gave me a demonstration of fencing moves. I liked the way he looked in that white jacket, the single leather glove on his right hand, but I wasn't so sure about the wire mesh mask. I thought it made him look like a huge insect. Or an executioner.

"Forget *The Three Musketeers*," he told me, "what you want to do is keep the blade within an imaginary frame around your body, to move as little as possible and still protect yourself. The most important part, though, is reading your opponent. It's like a game of chess, move and countermove," he said. "And when you get it just right, it's the best feeling in the world."

But as I watched him, so graceful on his feet as he advanced and then retreated, I thought it seemed less like a game than a strange and beautiful dance.

This second time, it was different. He wore no mask and his T-shirt was stained with sweat. There was a fierceness in his concentration, his brow furrowed, his lips pale. I don't even think he saw me at first. Again and again he lunged at his imaginary opponent: a feint to the chest, then the quick and fatal strike to the head. I could see the metal meet flesh, then the cold satisfaction in his eyes as he watched the body crumple to the floor. Whoever it was died several times over.

Finally he turned to me. He was too far away to touch me with the blade, but he extended his wrist toward me as if he were pointing me out to some unseen stranger.

I frowned. "Hey, watch out, you could hurt someone with that."

His mouth curved into a slight smile. "That's the idea," he said, tilting the saber back in salute.

I've been having troubles of my own. My father was in the hospital with another heart attack, and there was talk of surgery. The first time I went to visit, he came with me. As we walked through the corridors, the pallid fluorescent light and muted antiseptic smell began to make me feel ill, so I reached for his hand, the only warm, real thing in the whole place.

He waited in the hall while I went into the room. My father was sleeping. He looked so old, his face all creases and shadows. My mother was sitting by the bed staring down at the book on her lap. I glanced back at him, leaning against the wall across from the doorway, arms crossed, gazing straight ahead. His expression was patient, blank. I knew he didn't see me then. I wanted to be where he was—far, far away—but my mother pulled me back with her cool lips on my cheek, her anxious reassurances.

When she saw him, she stiffened, but, ever courteous, walked out to greet him. I watched them come together in a brief, guarded embrace; watched his lips move as he said something to her, watched her nod without really looking at him.

I'd known from the beginning that she didn't really approve of him. *Does he love you?* she asked me once, quietly, almost under her breath. I shrugged because that was the only answer I could give.

I wonder if she could have understood the attraction better if I had told her about the blindfold?

Strangely enough, one of my best ideas came from my mother. She was going through her sewing scrap box, when she pulled out a square of deep red velvet and said, "Remember this? It's from that dress I made you for Christmas when you were—how old—eight or nine?" The fabric was soft with age and I instinctively rubbed it over my hand, up over my wrist. It felt especially nice when I ran a velvet-covered finger along the inside of my arm. I was so lost in my sweet memories of that dress, how grown-up and glamorous I felt when I wore it to church on Christmas morning then over to my aunt's house for dinner, that I didn't realize for several moments that I held in my hand the perfect surprise for our next game.

It was a good one. After I blindfolded him, I had him lie face-down on the bed and guess what I was rubbing over his skin: the tip of my nose along his spine, the loose end of blindfold across his shoulders, my finger in the valley of his ass, my breasts across the back of his knees. I saved the velvet until last and stroked the length of him with it like I was polishing a precious, breakable object. He usually didn't make much noise when we made love, but by the time I was done with the back of him, he was almost mewing. And more than ready to turn over.

I dusted his chest and the discs of his nipples, then forced myself to linger at his belly, soothing the skin in small circles, ignoring his cock that reared up and twitched with each new caress. At last I wrapped the velvet around it and began to polish it like a newel post, with careful attention to the glossy knob. It was then I told him about the dress, about how I wore it with white tights and patent leather shoes and had a bow with holly on it in my hair, and about how thrilled I was when all of the adults told me I looked so pretty.

"I'll bet you were cute," he said with a smile as I lowered myself onto him and started my slow ride.

So cute, I told him, that even my oldest cousin—the one I had a crush on, the one who lives in Texas now—gallantly offered me a turn with his train set. Before I'd always had to beg and whine. But that day, I felt like a princess. And in trying to figure out what was different about it, I had my first inkling that the way to get something from boys is to look pretty. Then they'll do anything for you. "Isn't that true?" I asked him.

"Uh-huh," he replied, arching back into the pillow.

Not long after that he asked me to kneel when he put on the blindfold. Then he went on to position my body with his hands, telling me to keep my back straight, my shoulders down, my chin up. He told me not to move, not even to smile. He proceeded to caress me, starting at my cheeks just below the edge of the blindfold. He traced my lips with one fingertip, drew ovals on my chin, brushed my neck and collarbone with feathery strokes. I managed to hold myself still until his hands moved to my breasts. That's when he had to remind me of the rules and rearrange my body in the proper position. He even reprimanded me for breathing too quickly. "Slow, baby, nice and slow," he whispered, smoothing the tension from my lips and jaw until I was quiet.

But then he started up again, rolling my nipples between his fingers like he was fine-tuning a radio, rubbing one breast then the other with a spit-moistened palm. He knew my body. I had my proof then, if there was any doubt before. And all I could do was squeeze my eyes shut tighter and tighter under the blindfold as my cheeks began to burn and a fine sweat rose like lubricant on the skin beneath his hands. Soon my chest was throbbing so violently, my ribs ached. By then he'd moved down to my belly, drawing strange shapes that sometimes—just sometimes—extended farther down. Then he'd come back to tease my belly button with a wet finger, stroking, circling, slipping softly inside.

All the while my clit was growing heavy and hot. I imagined he could see it, poking out between my lips, flushed scarlet and shameless in its need. When he finally did touch it, I shuddered, earning me another scolding.

"Now, now. Don't you remember? Good girls keep still and quiet while their wet, swollen clits are being rubbed."

By then there was nothing I could do to stop myself from whimpering, *Please, oh, please, I think I'm gonna come*, but I guess the rules suddenly changed, because he pushed me back on the bed and entered me with an urgency that surprised me, that tiny part of me that was still capable of coherent thought. How could just touching me—a statue—excite him so much? But his breath was coming as fast as his thrusts, and I was not far behind.

The experience of orgasm in general is something I can easily conjure in my mind, but specific ones elude me. Even when I remember the circumstances of the lovemaking, the things we said and did, the climax blurs into a vague sensation of bliss. An ending. But that orgasm is one I still remember in my body, a searing rush of pleasure as my desire finally burst free, my skull blasted open to the rush of night wind, the chilled fire of the stars. And I remember marveling afterward that we had done it: we had found a way to make each time better than the last.

Of course it couldn't go on forever.

Earlier tonight I convinced him to watch an episode of an English TV series about a king with too many wives, because it was one of my favorite shows as a child. I had fond memories of sitting before the television with a notebook, sketching the Tudor gowns. But as I watched it again, I realized there was a lot I didn't remember. The growing sense of doom, the ugly marital quarrels, the political intrigue, the scene where the queen's musician was blinded under torture with a knotted rope. It was altogether too gloomy and talky, so I didn't complain when he started reading something halfway through. I decided to be satisfied he was there with me, idly rubbing my toes with one hand, holding the magazine with the other.

I noticed, however, that he started paying attention again when the queen was imprisoned on trumped up charges of adultery. When it got to the execution scene, he put down the magazine. And so we both watched, transfixed, as the queen glided over to the scaffold, made her poignant farewell speech, knelt down before the block. The lady-in-waiting tied a narrow, snow-white blindfold over the kneeling woman's eyes. In that one moment, before the sword, the actress looked more beautiful than ever, at least those parts of her set off by the blindfold above and the low-cut dress below: her pouting crimson lips, her fragile neck and the swelling of her breasts that rose and fell with each breath. I remembered something else from long ago, my brother and cousins in the back of the station wagon on a hot summer day, talking about that same television show. The only part of interest to them was when the queen "got her head chopped off." At the time, I didn't understand the edge of excitement in their voices.

But now I did.

We turn to each other with the same crooked, tight-lipped smiles.

"So, that was your favorite show?"

"Mmm," I reply. "I'd forgotten about that part."

We sit in silence.

Then I say to him, "What do you think goes through someone's mind at a time like that?"

He thinks, brow furrowed, then shakes his head.

More silence.

"So what do you want to do now?" I ask.

He shakes his head again. "I don't know. I'm in a weird mood."

I'm well aware that interesting things happen when he is in a weird mood.

I give him a sidelong glance. "Do you want to blindfold me?" I can't remember the last time we'd made love without it.

He looks at me curiously. "Now that would be too weird."

"But I want you to. I guess I'm in a weird mood, too. How about it?" I poke him.

"No," he replies sharply.

"How about 'yes'?" I say, taking up the challenge. I'll overcome his reluctance, make him want to do it. Before we had always glided into the game together, willingly, but I discover that this new element of conflict excites me.

He seems uneasy. "What's with you tonight?"

"What's with me? Who started this blindfold business anyway?"

"You didn't take much convincing, if I remember correctly."

This goes on for a while, until finally I ask, "Come on, what are you afraid of?"

That's when I know I've won, even before he stalks off to the bedroom and returns with the blindfold balled up in his fist.

"Should I get undressed?" I ask with a coy smile. I am still expecting him to smile back, still waiting for that flicker of desire in his eyes. It's always the last thing I see before the blindfold goes on.

But he just stares at me coldly. I've never seen him quite like this before.

I sit up. "Well, what should I do?"

"Just get down on your fucking knees."

He doesn't seem to be pretending. I know I'm not pretending when I jump, when my jaw falls open in surprise. I really am afraid of him. Afraid to meet his eyes. Afraid to breathe.

I stand up and look around the living room for a place to kneel. The coffee table takes up most of the well-worn oval rug, but there is plenty of scarred hardwood floor.

"Can I get a pillow or something?" I attempt another smile.

"Shut up and kneel," he says.

So, I kneel down and he ties the blindfold over my eyes.

The floor is hard and cold. I hear the tip-tap of his shoes as he leaves the room. I am alone. At first my mind is racing as I wonder what he could be doing. But then, as I wait in the stillness, with the blindfold on, I begin to feel safe. This darkness is familiar, with its memory and promise of pleasure, of yielding myself to him. The very air seems to press against me, heavy and faintly moist, the boundaries of my body softening with each breath.

Suddenly I hear footsteps behind me, a faint metallic clink. My shoulders tense, the air grows thin. Something very cool and smooth settles on the right side of my neck. In the next instant

I realize it is his hand. In a glove. A leather glove. It rests there
for a moment, the fingers gripping my throat. The leather grows
warm, sucking up the heat of my skin. Then it begins to move,
stroking my neck, brushing my cheek. I sigh.

"Do you like this?" His voice sounds far away.

I hesitate, afraid to get the answer wrong. "Yes."

"Then enjoy it while you can. Because after tonight I'll never
touch you again."

"What? What do you mean?"

"I mean, this is the last time."

His hand slips away.

"I don't understand. You're leaving me?"

"Don't worry, when it's all over, you won't care."

"What are you going to do?"

"Come on now." His voice is low, mocking as he turns my
own words against me. "What are you afraid of?"

I swallow hard.

It is fear, this tightness in my chest, the tingling where my neck
curves into my shoulder, the very place a blade would strike.

But he wouldn't really go that far, would he?

Maybe he just enjoys watching me like this, the way my
breasts quiver with each gasp and my lips part in an O as if I'm
about to come. It would be more like him to tease me with the
saber, ease the cool metal up between my thighs so I'm forced
to ride it, avoiding the edges with exquisite care. He might even
hold it to my neck as he pushes his cock into me and whispers
The last time, the last time, the words alone awakening hot ten-
drils of pleasure deep inside my cunt. And the ending would be
sweet: no slow, gray withering, but a flash of silver behind my
eyelids, a crimson flush rolling across my skin, a princess suspended in the prime of her beauty.

"This is part of the game, right?" My voice is pleading, hopeful.

At first he doesn't reply. I hear the floorboards creak, another clink of metal. Footsteps circle around to my left and stop somewhere in front of me. Then he snorts, a soft hiss of air. "Don't you see I'm tired of playing your sick games?"

My games?

For a moment I am aware of nothing but a coldness spreading up through my chest, down my arms, settling in my fingers as a dull, distant ache.

But suddenly I do see it, hovering against the blindfold: the image of myself as he really sees me now, as he must have seen me all along. A body—exposed and vulnerable, but not beautiful, not beloved.

"Why are you doing this to me?" I cry out, half-choking on the words as I collapse to the floor, chest sagging onto my knees. I don't want to cry, not in front of him, not now, so I press my palms over my eyes, but the tears come anyway, stinging as they rise, spilling over into the silk.

Hands grasp my shoulders. I twist away instinctively, but they hold me fast, and I begin to feel, through the cloth of my shirt, the warmth of skin, a gentleness in his fingers. Then he pulls me up, murmuring something I can't hear through my own sobs. I struggle to my feet and bury my face in his shoulder. He strokes my back, swaying.

As I cling to him, I say less in accusation than wonder, "You were torturing me. Do you see that?"

"Isn't it what you wanted?" he whispers.

"No. I don't think so. I don't know," I say. In truth, I don't think I'd ever really been aware of what I was asking him to do.

"Believe me, I didn't mean to hurt you. I never want to hurt you." His arms tighten around me, squeezing me with a force just short of actual pain.

It is the blindfold that suddenly seems unbearably tight.

"Take it off now. Please?" I could pull it off myself—it has always been a voluntary bondage—but I want him to do it. I want him to break the spell.

His hands fumble at the knot. Then he pulls the scarf free and lets it fall to the floor.

I look up and see that his eyes are wet too, like wounds. I lean toward him. He closes his eyes, and so do I, an unthinking act that all lovers do. In that simple darkness we find each other's lips. I want at this moment nothing more than the exquisitely ordinary comfort of his lips against mine.

It is enough.

FIRST
THINGS FIRST

Stephen Elliott

The Grasshopper youth hostel in Amsterdam was three stories high and appeared like an old red brick mansion rising over the third canal. Green lights climbed the walls like vines and gargoyles perched on the corners, their talons digging into the cement. It cost eight dollars a night to bunk in dorm rooms with twenty beds and was located on the Warmoesstraat, near the Old Church and the Terminus where the streets were slick with vomit, beer, and urine.

Outside everything was for sale and pickpockets followed you watching to see where you held your wallet. There was always a party at night, neon marijuana leaves in the windows, gays in chaps and shirtless women cruising out front. Junkies sat on bags of garbage sticking their arms. Near the bridges students played guitar while their friends waved hats and asked for change.

There were jugglers and sex shows and the authorities had not yet cracked down on the illegal immigrants sitting in lingerie in rented doorways along the Oudezijds.

The clerk at the Grasshopper was a large Moroccan with a helmet of curly black hair. He was arguing with two men in the entrance. They wanted to see one of the hostel tenants.

"He's not here," the clerk said. He sounded impatient. If he turned to reach the phone one of them would slip past to the upper floors.

"That's impossible he isn't here," the smaller one told the clerk as if speaking to a child. "Because he owes us money."

One of the men arguing at the counter turned and stared at me, sizing me up, weighing my value while his friend pleaded their case. His friend hammered his fist on the counter. "Get out," the man behind the counter said.

"Look at him," the smaller one said to me, baring his teeth, spittle gathering in the corner of his mouth. "He doesn't understand. Why not?"

A woman stood near the yellow lockers with a magazine in her hand and a bored expression on her face. She was old compared to me, and not pretty. I was only twenty, and traveling on a one-way ticket. She had thick shoulders, a football player's body, and short spiky hair that had gone gray in patches. If her face wasn't so weathered and pockmarked and sturdy it might have resembled a young boy's. She wore black boots and a leather skirt without stockings. Her skin was the color of clay.

I paused for a moment on the bottom stair, then approached the woman and told her I had seen her earlier at the bar on the end of the canal. There were rules at that bar for what people could and could not wear so I had not worn a shirt. I sat half naked in the corner in a deep black chair and drank a Coke. She had been on a platform at the far end torturing a red-haired man. His arms were chained above his head and he was blindfolded. He had a pointy beard; his body was soft and shapeless, impossible to see where his chest ended and his stomach began. She had covered him in clothespins, which she twisted and squeezed.

"I don't remember you," she said. I smiled and looked at the floor, trying to hide my panic. "I think I would remember you. What were you doing in that bar?" she asked.

The man near the counter turned his attention back to the clerk.

Outside was cold. I walked with her to her hotel. I don't think she gave me her name but if she did I forgot it right away. "You should have a scarf in this weather," she told me.

We walked across the bridges and down the Voorburg to where the lights ended. I was glad to be away from the men at the counter. I felt safe with this woman because she was Dutch and her body was so sturdy. I didn't ask her what she was doing in the youth hostel. She told me she wasn't from Amsterdam; she lived somewhere near Rotterdam. She had come to Amsterdam for a party, and she asked, if I knew about the party that was going to happen in a couple of days. "A big event," she said.

I told her I didn't know about it.

The Royal Kabul was on the edge of the red-light district, just past the Moulin Rouge and the sex museum, near the Zeedijk. The streets around the hotel were very quiet and all of the windows facing the street were dark. I stopped at the entrance, my hands tucked in my pockets. I was scared that she would tell me I couldn't come in with her and I would have to walk back. There was no safe way back to the hostel at night. Along the canal was a low green rail and people were pushed over sometimes and beaten when they climbed out wet on the other side. She knew what she wanted to do but she let a few moments pass. "You can come into the bar and I'll buy you a drink. But you'll have to dance for me." Which is what I did. I danced for her.

I danced with my eyes closed a couple of feet away from her

while she sat on a stool with a glass of rum. There was a beer next to her but when I tried to pick it up she said, "No, dance first." I worried a little that if I danced too far away one of the hotel managers would collar me, and demand to see my room key, which of course I didn't have. I thought if I was behind other people, and she couldn't see me, then she wouldn't notice them walking me out with their hands on my elbows and the back of my neck and I knew she wouldn't come looking for me. She would see I was gone and presume I had just run off, changed my mind. Nobody ever looks for you when you disappear except on television. In real life they let you go and then forget. She would shrug her shoulders and go back to her room and I would be left to my own devices. So I stayed close, as close as I could, and when I got close enough she reached out and grabbed me by my belt and pulled me forward so I was dancing over her leg and she put her hand on my ass and whispered, "I think you and I might have some things in common." Then she pinched my earlobe and I let out a quick yelp.

In her room she was very formal. There was a dresser and a black case and a window with the curtain pulled. She didn't ask what I liked, which was good because I had no idea what I liked or what I was into or what I wanted to do or wanted done to me. "Take your clothes off and put them in the corner. Come on." She snapped her fingers beneath my nose. She seemed to think I had been through this before, but I hadn't. I had been arrested as a child and I spent three months in a mental hospital when I was fourteen, but that was all. "Raise your arms, spread your legs, turn around." She ran her hands over my arms and between my legs, searching me until she was satisfied. She tied me to the bed faceup with rope and rubber straps and pulled a hood over my head so I couldn't see anything. There was a hole for my mouth. She tied my cock and balls together and told me to stick my tongue out and then slapped my face hard, the way my father used to. "Stick your tongue out further," she said. "Good. Stay like that."

I knew it was a knife right away, as soon as I felt the cold on my leg. She had run a rope over my neck so I couldn't lift my head. I felt the knife working its way across my body, not quite cutting me. I knew the knife was sharp, I felt my skin wanting to break. Then I felt the first cut. "Just a little blood," she said. "For me." She drew the knife below my penis and lifted my balls with the flat side of the blade. All of my muscles tensed and I started to cry inside the hood.

"Relax," she said. "There's nothing you can do one way or the other. Breathe." She waited but I couldn't catch my breath. She pulled the knife away, then gripped my balls tightly in her fist and I screamed.

"I said breathe. Breathe for your mommy." I tried to focus. I tried to breathe, and I finally did, I breathed in large, deep breaths, and she loosened her grip. I thought of the couch in the living room where I grew up and my mother lying there under a knit blanket for many years. "That's better. That's what mommy wants. You only have a couple of cuts on your leg and you're crying already. Now I'm going to put something in your mouth so you don't scream again."

I didn't know anything about safewords then. She peeled the hood to just below my nose. The gag was a large plastic puck with a hole in the center of it and it stretched my cheeks painfully and hurt more still when she pulled the hood back over my face. I heard the snap of the lighter and smelled the smoke. First her finger poked through the mouth hole in the mask and the puck and she ran her fingernail over my tongue, pressed it down. Then she flicked the ashes in my mouth. I could hear the paper burn away at the edges every time she took a drag and

I was only able to moan like some doomed animal when she lowered the finished cigarette onto my ribs, dotting it out across my skin.

At some point, it may have been hours, she untied me and plucked the gag from my cheeks. I was very weak and tired and my body was shaking involuntarily and she turned me over. "Onto your knees," she said. "Like a puppy dog. That's a good boy." She placed pillows beneath my stomach and smeared me in Vaseline and she entered me from behind with her strap-on. She did it slowly, very slowly, and it didn't hurt as much as it might have. I had never been entered before. She leaned across my back, wrapping one arm around my chest and gripping my neck with her other hand, occasionally squeezing my windpipe so I couldn't breathe for a second. I cried again, but it was a different crying. I was very comfortable. I don't think I had ever been comfortable before. She rubbed her hand over my face, washing my cheeks with my tears. "Yes," she said. "Cry some more. I like that very much." When she was done I slept curled in a ball facing her, my forehead against her collarbone, her heavy arm across my shoulder.

Early in the morning, while the city was still dark, I got dressed and shouldered my pack. I pushed the curtain and saw a deep red over the tops of the buildings like the edge of a bruise. I couldn't go back to America. I didn't know where I could go. I opened the leather case and saw all of the sharp tools, gags, dildos, wrist cuffs, chains, iodine, needles, latex gloves, and several hundred dollars. She was sleeping and I considered taking her money. I had already robbed a man who had taken me home in London. We'd met at an upscale bar in Chelsea, there was a strip contest and the winner received the loudest applause from the crowd. "Cheer for me," I told him, before stepping onto the podium, but all he did was clap politely as I stripped to my underwear, so I lost. He said he was a chef for the French Embassy and I went home with him but I asked him not to touch me. I said there would be time for that later but I was just stalling. I took a wool sweater from him and a small pile of twenty-pound notes.

She was still wearing her boots and leather skirt and sleeping peacefully. I watched her sleeping for a while. I didn't know anything about her except that she was heavy, too heavy to lift, and she lived somewhere else. I closed the case and bit my lip. I didn't understand what I was feeling. I thought it was an urge to be buried alive or drowned but it was probably a desire to crawl back into bed and stay.

I left and I walked straight to the Terminus and boarded a train to Berlin. In Berlin I rented a very small room just east of the wall, which had been torn down recently. People were painting all over the sides of buildings, giant murals everywhere. I sat in that room in East Berlin for two weeks listening to German radio and sleeping and masturbating until my penis was lined with friction sores and broken skin. When I finally made it back to Amsterdam I couldn't find her. Holland is a small country but I wasn't from there. I went to the Royal Kabul but I didn't even have her name. She didn't live there. She was gone.

THE KISS

Alison Tyler

The waiter's watching you."

"What do you mean?"

Jack leaned in closer to my ear. "He's looking at you. Every time he goes by our table. He thinks he's being sly, but…"

As he spoke, I turned my head to look at the waiter he was talking about, a lean dark-eyed man who made unexpectedly forceful eye contact with me, who held my gaze for a beat too long.

"See?" Jack murmured.

"I didn't do anything…" I started in my defense.

"Ah, Carla, I didn't say you did. But I want you to."

I turned to face him. What did he have in mind?

"Just enter into a little flirtatious banter with him," Jack said. "With your eyes. You know how to do it. I'm sure you do."

"Come on, Jack."

"Are you disobeying me?"

I went instantly pink. "No, of course not…"

"Then do as I say. I want to see you flirt. I want to know

what you look like when you're making eyes at another man."

Each time the waiter brought us a new plate of food, or refilled our wine glasses, or stopped by simply to check our status, I felt his eyes roam over me. Jack had one hand on my thigh under the table, and he kept a steady pressure on my leg, squeezing tightly, wanting me to do as he'd requested.

I tried hard. With Jack right next to me, flirting felt impossible. But I did my best. I shot the dark-haired boy my infamous coy, up-from-under glances. I felt rusty, but apparently my tricks worked just fine. He seemed mesmerized.

When the after-dinner drinks arrived, Jack put his hand on the side of my neck, his fingertips stroking my bare skin. "The bathrooms are upstairs. Go on up. I'm sure he'll follow you."

"Jack?"

"Get him to kiss you..."

"Come on, Jack..."

"Get him to kiss you up there. That's all. Nothing more than that. Just a kiss. Then come back to the table and have your drink like nothing ever happened."

We'd killed a bottle of wine with dinner, and I felt shaky as I made my way through the restaurant and up the tiny stairs to the landing. There was a pay phone next to a mirrored wall, prints by Toulouse Lautrec, and two bathroom doors. I hesitated in front of the mirror, fixing my hair, when the waiter came upstairs.

He looked at me and I smiled, shocked at how right Jack had been. The man started to speak, and I somehow knew what he was going to say before I heard the words "So sexy..." and I shook my head and took a step forward. It was all I had to do. He pressed me back against the mirrored wall and kissed me. I could sense how hard he was through his black slacks, could smell his aftershave, could feel the start of his evening beard scrape my cheek. He tried to bring his hands up to my breasts, but I grabbed onto them instead and held them at his sides. Jack said to kiss. That was all. The feel of this stranger's mouth on mine sent a powerful shock through me. He kissed so differently from Jack. Soft and slow at first, then all consuming. I let the pleasure build within me, and then I pulled back and smiled at him.

"I can't..." I said. "I can't do any more..." and I turned and hurried into the ladies' room, intent on fixing my hair, my smudged lipstick.

Jack was waiting impatiently when I came back downstairs. The table was cleared, the bill was gone. We took a cab back to the hotel, and he didn't speak a word the whole ride.

I wondered if I had failed. If the test hadn't been about my obedience in this case, but my refusal. Fear flickered through me, and I felt lost, until Jack gripped my wrist and led me to the elevators. And suddenly I understood. I had done what he said. To the very last degree. And now he was going to punish me for it....

"What did it feel like?" Jack asked me.

"I was nervous."

"Sure, but what did the kiss feel like...?"

I closed my eyes, trying to recreate every minute detail. "His lips were soft," I started, "and I could tell that he was a smoker, because he had that taste of tobacco." This isn't a bad thing to me. My first boyfriend back in high school smoked Marlboros, and one of my most intense memories is the way his kisses sometimes tasted of smoke.

Jack took my wrists in his hands and gently clicked the cuffs into place. I was bound faceup on the hotel bed, with my ankles spread and attached to the metal frame under the mattress.

"More—" he said, pressing me. "Tell me more."

"I could hear the patrons downstairs," I told him, "and I thought about you sipping your drink...."

"I don't believe you kissed him." Jack now held a flogger in one hand, and he traced the many fine ends along my ribs, tickling me. "I think you pretended to make a call, you stayed with your back to him, you didn't even look in his direction."

I took a deep breath, trying to figure out how to prove myself. "He was wearing some spicy cologne," I started, trying again. "His lips were soft and he pressed them firmly to mine, and then slowly parted them and touched my tongue with his...."

Jack changed tactics suddenly, surprisingly. "How do I know you didn't fuck him?"

He'd gone from disbelief that I'd engaged in a kiss, to certainty that I'd taken off my panties, and I panicked.

"I didn't, Jack. God, of course I didn't." What could I say? "You can tell. Touch me, there. Come on... You could tell if I'd been with another man."

"Keep describing what happened."

"I gripped his hands and held them to his sides when he tried to touch my breasts. I just kissed him, Jack. That was all. Just like you told me."

The flogger danced along my body, landing once, sharply, between my legs. I shuddered but didn't beg. Didn't cry out.

Jack was in motion now, the weapon graceful in his grip, crisscrossing the blows over that most tender skin. I could feel the strokes as they built in intensity. He started lightly, but worked gradually up until my hips were squirming on the mattress. There was almost no give in the way he'd bound me, but I could raise and lower my hips, could beg with the motions of my body.

I understood why he was punishing me. This time it was for obeying him. I'd never done anything like this before—kissing another man at the request of my boyfriend. Yeah, I'd cheated on my ex. But not with his permission. I thought about the pleasure I'd gotten from meeting my lovers on the sly—kissing them, fucking them—and then returning home to my ex. This was nothing like that emotion. I'd kissed the waiter only because Jack had told me to.

"Would you have fucked him?" The flogger was gone, on the floor, and Jack was bent by my feet, undoing the bindings.

"No, Jack, no—"

"If I'd told you to go upstairs and take off your panties and wait for him, would you have obeyed me?"

Ah, Jesus. It was a trap. I'd fallen in. I'd failed.

"No, Jack…" He was turning me, now, facedown on the bed. My pussy throbbed from the flogging, but I knew that had been a mere wake-up call to whatever he had planned next.

"You'd have disobeyed me?"

A trick. A cruel Dom trick.

"I don't want to fuck anyone else, Jack."

"But you *did* want to kiss him?"

I turned my head, looking up at him over my shoulder. I felt helpless. "Please—"

"Please, what, baby?" He was right next to me, his mouth so close. "Please kiss you? Like you kissed him?"

I was screwed. I got that now. If I'd disobeyed in the restaurant, he would have undoubtedly spanked me right there, in public, as he had threatened in the past. So I had done what he'd told me. But if he had said to fuck the waiter, I would not have obeyed. I'd have begged him, pleaded. I would have done whatever he said in order to please him in a different manner. There was a line I was unwilling to cross. Jack was illuminating that line for me.

"Slut," Jack said under his breath, standing once more. I watched him undo his belt. I waited for him to strike. Instead, he brought the buckle up to my lips. He waited for me to kiss it. Just the concept of kissing now felt tainted. "I'm not going to give you the gag tonight," Jack said. "You're going to have to keep yourself quiet."

He took his time. He worked me hard. The buckle caught my skin every few blows, and I knew those bruises were going to last. I cried. Tears streaking my face. Wetting the pillow. But I did not scream. I did not fight.

I had failed him.

By obeying, I had failed.

I deserved whatever he had to give me.

I was sure he would leave me tied all night. That he might even leave the room. I prepared myself for that eventuality. Hoping that I would behave in a manner that would please him. So when he stripped off his clothes, I was surprised.

Jack left me tied. I had that part right. And he spit on his fingertips and worked that wetness around my hole. He fucked me as hard as he'd whipped me, taking my ass with an almost frightening intensity.

And when he was done, he still kept me tied, but he didn't leave the room. He wrapped his body around mine, and held me like that.

"You can't always win," he whispered. "There was no way tonight for you to win. It was a losing proposition from the start." He lifted my dark hair off my neck and blew his breath against me.

I thought of my roommate's print of *The Kiss* on the wall of my college dorm. I thought of Lisa cooing about the sexiness of the image, how it would be so divine to have a man kiss you like that. And I turned my head and met Jack's eyes as he finally kissed me for the first time that night. Really kissed me.

Divine.

ABOUT THE
AUTHORS

LISETTE ASHTON is a UK author who has published more than two dozen erotic novels and countless short stories. Written principally for Virgin's Nexus imprint, as well as occasionally writing for the CP label Chimera Publishing, Lisette Ashton's stories have been described by reviewers as "no-holds-barred naughtiness" and "good dirty fun."

VIDA BAILEY is a teacher who would much rather be a writer. She lives in Ireland with her husband, daughter and Internet habit. This is her first published piece.

RACHEL KRAMER BUSSEL (www.rachelkramerbussel.com) is senior editor at *Penthouse Variations*. She's the editor or co-editor of thirteen erotic anthologies, including *Caught Looking: Erotic Tales of Voyeurs and Exhibitionists, He's on Top: Erotic Stories of Male Dominance and Female Submission* and *She's on Top: Erotic Stories of Female Dominance and Male Submission*

(Cleis Press), and *Naughty Spanking Stories from A to Z 1* and *2* (Pretty Things Press), and her stories have been published in over ninety anthologies, including *Best American Erotica 2004* and *2006*. Rachel is currently completing her first novel, *Everything But...*, to be published by Bantam in 2008.

JEN CROSS' writing can be found in such publications as *Naughty Spanking Stories A-Z, Volume 2, Nobody Passes, Best Women's Erotica 2007*, on CleanSheets.com, and in the forthcoming *Fantasy: Untrue Stories of Lesbian Passion*. She is currently working on two book-length collections. A queer survivor of sexual abuse, she's a firm believer in the transformative potential of smut. For more information about Jen and her work, including her writing workshops, visit www.writingourselveswhole.org.

STEPHEN ELLIOTT is the author of six books including *Happy Baby* and *My Girlfriend Comes to the City and Beats Me Up*.

RYAN FIELD is a thirty-five-year-old freelance writer who lives and works in both Bucks County, PA and Los Angeles, CA. His short stories have been published in many gay anthologies and collections, and at the present time he's working on a novel. He also interviews and writes about gay bloggers for www.bestgayblogs.com, where he's working on a nonfiction book that involves the cathartic process of blogging.

SHANNA GERMAIN looks like the girl next door, but she doubts you'd want to live next to her. Her writing has been widely published in places like *Absinthe Literary Review, Best American Erotica, Best Bondage Erotica, Caught Looking,* and *D Is for Dress-Up*. You can read more of her work online at www.shannagermain.com.

TERESA LAMAI's erotic stories have appeared in several anthologies, including *Best Lesbian Romance, Best Women's Erotica, Best Lesbian Erotica, Lips Like Sugar: Women's Erotic Fantasies, Dying for It: Stories of Sex and Death, Mammoth Book of Best New Erotica,* and *Zane's Caramel Flava.* Her novella *Planet Justine* will soon be available from Mojocastle Press.

JAMES WALTON LANGOLF smiles sweetly and says, "Hey, there stranger, come meet a girl. She's usually unusual, a funny little mystery, a charming curiosity, a pretty blue-eyed girl named James living a beautiful life in sunny Arizona. She drinks too much and never eats or sleeps enough. She laughs far too loud and sweetens everything (even her words when she can) with clover honey." Contact her at jameswlangolf@gmail.com.

KRISTINA LLOYD is the author of three erotic novels, *Darker Than Love, Asking for Trouble,* and *Split,* all published by Black Lace. She has a first-class degree and a masters in English literature and lives for a good story. She lives in Brighton on the south coast of England, and prefers the beach in winter to summer. She listens to Tom Waits too much, and loves worlds that are skewed and sleazy.

NIKKI MAGENNIS lives, loves and works in the city of Glasgow, Scotland. After training as an artist she accidentally fell into writing erotica, and is having a marvelous time. Her first novel, *Circus Excite,* was published by Black Lace in 2006, and you can find her short stories in *Sex and Music, Sex in Public,* and the forthcoming *Sex with a Stranger* (all Black Lace publications). Get a glimpse into her world at: http://nikkimagennis.blogspot.com.

SOMMER MARSDEN's work has appeared in numerous e-zines including Clean Sheets and Oysters and Chocolate. She is a regular contributor to Ruthie's Club and The Erotic Woman. Most recent print credits include *The MILF Anthology* and *Sultry Shades of Christmas*. She lives in Maryland and can be reached at best_little_secrets@hotmail.com. Sommer is too lazy to build a website so updates and blogs can be found at www.myspace.com/sommermarsden.

ZAEDRYN MEADE is a self-defined sugarbutch whose erotica has been published in *Penitalia: Collegiate Erotica, Best Lesbian Erotica 2006* and *2007, Second Skin,* and *Secret Slaves: Erotic Stories of Bondage.* Born in Southeast Alaska, she now lives in New York City.

BROOKE STERN is the pseudonym of an established writer whose fiction, essays and reviews have been published widely and translated into eight languages. "The Art of the Suture" is adapted from a story in *Bad Girls* (Chimera Books), a short-story collection. You can read more of Brooke Stern's erotica in *Naughty Spanking Stories from A to Z, Volume 2* (Pretty Things Press), *Bonds of Love* (Magic Carpet Books), as well as *A Is for Amour* and *C Is for Coed* (both Cleis). Email: brooke.stern@gmail.com.

DONNA GEORGE STOREY's erotic fiction has appeared in *She's On Top: Stories of Female Dominance and Male Submission, He's On Top: Stories of Male Dominance and Female Submission, Garden of the Perverse: Fairy Tales for Twisted Adults, Taboo: Forbidden Fantasies for Couples, Best American Erotica 2006, Mammoth Book of Best New Erotica 4, 5* and *6,* and *Best Women's Erotica 2005, 2006,* and *2007.* Her novel set in Japan,

Amorous Woman, is part of Orion's Neon erotica series. Read more of her work at www.DonnaGeorgeStorey.com.

XAN WEST is the pseudonym of an NYC BDSM activist and teacher whose current project is an S/M nonfiction book for survivors of trauma. Xan's story "Dancing for Daddy" was published in *Best S/M Erotica 2.* Xan enjoys vampires, writing, boots, magick, knives, punching, and fucking with gender. Xan can be reached at xan_west@yahoo.com.

ABOUT THE EDITOR

Called a "literary siren" by *Good Vibrations*, Alison Tyler is naughty and she knows it. She is the author of more than twenty explicit novels, including *Rumors*, *Tiffany Twisted*, and *With or Without You* (all published by Cheek), and the winner of "best kinky sex scene" as awarded by *Scarlet Magazine*. Her novels and short stories have been translated into Japanese, Dutch, German, Italian, Norwegian, Greek, and Spanish.

According to Clean Sheets, "Alison Tyler has introduced readers to some of the hottest contemporary erotica around." And she's done so through the editing of more than thirty sexy anthologies, including the *Naughty Stories from A to Z* series, the *Down & Dirty* series, *Naked Erotica* and *Juicy Erotica* (all from Pretty Things Press). Please drop by www.prettythingspress.com.

Ms. Tyler is loyal to coffee (black), lipstick (red), and tequila (straight). She has tattoos, but no piercings; a wicked tongue, but a quick smile; and bittersweet memories, but no regrets. She believes it won't rain if she doesn't bring an umbrella, prefers hot and dry to cold and wet, and loves to spout her favorite motto: "You can sleep when you're dead." She chooses Led Zeppelin over the Beatles, the Cure over NIN, and the Stones over everyone—yet although she appreciates good rock, she has a pitiful weakness for '80s hair bands. In all things important, she remains faithful to her partner of more than a decade, but she still can't settle on one perfume.

Visit www.alisontyler.com for more luscious revelations or myspace.com/alisontyler if you'd like to be her friend.